DOLLS *of* HOPE

SHIRLEY PARENTEAU

CANDLEWICK PRESS

This is a work of fiction. Names, characters, places, and incidents are either products of the author's imagination or, if real, are used fictitiously.

First edition 2015

Library of Congress Catalog Card Number 2014954534
ISBN 978-0-7636-7752-7

15 16 17 18 19 20 BVG 10 9 8 7 6 5 4 3 2 1

Printed in Berryville, VA, U.S.A.

This book was typeset in Walbaum.

Candlewick Press
99 Dover Street
Somerville, Massachusetts 02144

visit us at www.candlewick.com

For my daughter-in-law, Miwa,
with warm thanks for her gentle
corrections and generous advice.

For my granddaughters Michelle and Nicole
for sharing their beautiful photos
posed in kimonos for Hinamatsuri.

And with love always for my husband, Bill.

••••

I'd also like to thank everyone at Candlewick
who helped bring Chiyo's story to life,
especially my wise editor, Sarah Ketchersid,
and marketing assistant Sawako Shirota,
who coincidentally spent her early years in
Tsuchiura, where much of this story takes place,
and whose suggestions are greatly appreciated.

CHAPTER 1

Foothills Northwest of Tokyo
February 1927

Breathless with possibility, eleven-year-old Chiyo clung to the side of her father's oxcart. A big wicker basket tied in the back usually carried bamboo wind chimes her father made to sell at village festivals. It would be easy to climb inside and pull the lid over her head. She could ride unseen to the *omiai* with her seventeen-year-old sister and their parents. She could see the widowed man who had arranged to marry Masako.

No one would even know I'm there. The risk tantalized her. None of the family really knew Yamada Nori. Chiyo longed to investigate him. In secret.

"He's too old and lives too far away," Chiyo said aloud to the ox. She glared into the animal's soft brown eyes. "Lie down! Refuse to get up! Do not take my sister and parents behind that rich man's high walls."

The ox turned its head as if to say it was only an ox and must do as its master ordered.

Masako called from the doorway, "Chiyo-chan, I am to be married, not taken prisoner."

"You may cry every day behind Yamada Nori's locked gate," Chiyo warned. "We will be too far away to know."

Masako's eyes shone. Chiyo thought she looked more like five than seventeen. "That is why the marriage broker arranged the *omiai* tonight. When *Otousan*, *Okaasan*, and I meet Yamada-san over the formal dinner, we will learn if we should object to the arranged marriage."

From the glow in Masako's eyes, Chiyo didn't think her sister would notice if Yamada Nori's big house was on fire. Would their parents? "I would notice anything wrong."

"You!" Masako teased. "Younger sisters never attend an *omiai*. You might steal his attention from me!" Her smile became gentle. "You have your friend Yumi and her little sister, Kimi, to play with. You won't be alone when I marry, Chiyo-chan. Look, I am giving you Momo."

Chiyo reluctantly accepted the little doll shaped like a column with a round head. She had only one doll of her own, another wooden *kokeshi*. Masako's Momo had a prettier kimono painted on her limbless body and a sweeter smile. But owning Momo wouldn't make up for losing her sister.

"Masako," their mother called from inside the house. "We must finish your hair. We will leave soon."

"You should marry a man from our mountain village so we can visit you," Chiyo called as her sister rushed inside. Masako didn't answer. She was determined to travel down to richer land where Yamada Nori hired men and women to work his vast rice fields.

To the ox, Chiyo said, "My sister is making a terrible mistake."

The ox mooed in its low voice, clearly agreeing with her, and drawing Chiyo's attention back to the basket. If she did go—if she hid in the basket—she could slip through the dark and learn what Yamada Nori kept behind his high walls.

She might see something frightening for Masako and warn their parents. At the very least, she would see where her sister was to live. Then she could picture her sister's life when they were separated and feel Masako close in her heart.

She climbed onto the side of the wagon and hesitated. She was risking her honor, but she reminded herself softly, "No one will ever know if Masako is miserable once those high gates close behind her!"

Her parents and sister were coming. The sound of their voices rushed Chiyo over the side of the cart and into the basket. When she lowered the lid, darkness closed around her. She smelled nothing but wicker and, more faintly, the scent of bamboo.

The clatter of *geta* told Chiyo that her family had reached the wagon. She knew they wore their finest kimonos. The cart swayed as they climbed onto the bench seat behind the ox.

Again, her conscience prodded. All her life, she had been told that honor was everything. She could still call out that she had only been pretending to go with them.

Instead, she braced herself in the jolting basket

as the ox started forward down the winter-damaged road. Streams crossed in many places, carrying spring melt and washing out small crevices. The ride would not be easy for those on the bench seat, but even if the basket turned on its side, she would not make a sound.

She heard her mother say with gentle approval, "Our daughter has captured the heart of a wealthy man. May he also be kind."

Masako's voice held nothing but confidence. "He is kind, *Okaasan.* While I worked among the others from our village harvesting his rice, none were whipped and all were treated fairly."

Her father sounded strained. "He is more than twice your age, with two half-grown daughters in school in Osaka."

Too old, Chiyo thought, but her mother spoke gently. "Do not fear, daughter. *Otousan* knows this is a fine match. He will not let doubts cause Yamada-san to question the marriage."

Their father did not answer, though he must have known that the words were meant for him.

A smile sounded in *Okaasan*'s voice as she added, "No man is worthy of our daughter in our eyes, my husband. We are fortunate that such an excellent man has looked favorably on Masako."

Silently, Chiyo rebelled. True, Masako would live in a grand house with servants to tie her obi and *obi-jime*. She would have more elaborately patterned kimonos than ever before and so much fine food that she would never again be hungry.

But that was not the same as a loving, happy family. What if those two daughters did not wish for a new mother? They could make life horrible for Masako. And she did not love Yamada Nori. She had never even spoken to him, simply worked in his fields. He had noticed her. Of course he had. Masako was a hard worker and the prettiest young woman in their village.

The cart jolted over a large rock, slamming the basket up, then down. Chiyo bit her lip but didn't make a sound. She braced more carefully against the sides.

Although the cart rolled and jolted behind the plodding ox, Chiyo almost dozed and came fully awake only when the way became smooth. *Otousan* said, "Here is the border of Yamada Nori's property."

"He does well to keep the road between his boundaries free of winter damage," *Okaasan* replied with approval.

Chiyo's father was not as impressed. "He would

do even better to smooth the road before and beyond."

"Surely there is no need to repair property that is not his own," Masako dared to say.

Chiyo was not surprised when her father's answer was sharp. He was not used to his daughters questioning him. "I spoke of a thoughtful gesture to his neighbors. Be careful, elder daughter. While we are here, do not speak unless spoken to."

"Yes, *Otousan.*" Masako answered so softly she could barely be heard. Was her sister to lose herself when she married?

"The open gate welcomes us," *Okaasan* said.

Too curious to be still, Chiyo lifted the basket lid just enough to peer beneath as a servant led the oxcart through the gate. Her lips parted on a quick, startled breath.

CHAPTER 2

The large house looked like a bright chain of festival lanterns. Light shining through translucent shoji screens gleamed over black stepping-stones freshly washed in welcome and the dark glimmer of ponds set into the lawn.

Yamada Nori stood silhouetted in the open doorway. To Chiyo, the gleaming stones formed an arrow pointing straight at the owner. He could be no one else. Even the way he stood commanded attention. He owned the house, the ponds, and all the land around. One glance at him told her that. *He is dangerous,* she thought. *Masako should stay away from him.*

She lowered the basket lid silently while her family exchanged greetings with Yamada-san. They had joined him at the entry and, from the sound of their voices, were walking with him into the house.

Chiyo reached for the basket lid, but a servant murmured to the ox, and the cart moved again. Soon the animal's hooves clattered over a stone floor. Nearby, a horse whickered. A horse! Few people kept an animal so expensive to feed and maintain, yet Yamada Nori owned one. Chiyo risked raising the lid again and discovered that the cart had been led into an open shed.

From the sounds it was making, the ox now grazed happily on a mound of hay. A single lamp cast a glow of light, enough for her to see the horse peering curiously over a wooden barrier. Where was the servant? She listened hard and just made out footsteps moving away.

It was hard to wait, but she stayed silent in the basket for a few minutes longer while the ox chewed noisily and occasionally the horse shifted in the stall. At last, she climbed from the basket and eased from the cart to the stone floor. Even the back of the house glowed with light. She no longer saw a festival lantern. Now she saw a demon with fiery eyes.

She must learn the truth about this place. And about Yamada Nori.

After a quick glance in every direction, she crossed a lit area to try to see into the nearest room. Like a moth, she moved from glowing screen to glowing screen, working her way down the back of the house and along one side to the front.

At last, she stood beside a stone lantern, looking past a partially open screen into a room where a polished table stood on short legs above glowing tatami mats. Her family sat there with Yamada-san, all of them on low cushions, while they enjoyed the first part of their meal.

Masako took tiny bites, as if she feared she might be asked a question and dared not be caught with her mouth full. At home, Masako ate quickly, as they all did. None of the family had time to waste over food.

Strong hands grabbed the back of Chiyo's kimono. Choking, she fought to loosen the cloth at her throat. A man's voice exclaimed, "Now I have you! Let us see how Yamada-san deals with intruders."

The servant pushed her ahead of him into the house, pausing only for her to slip off her shoes and place them by the door. She heard again her mother's warning that none of them must shame the family, that Yamada-san must not have cause to change his mind about the marriage. The enormity of what she had done crashed over her.

Her family would never forgive her. Masako would hate her. She had ruined her sister's life. And her own.

Shame overwhelmed her. There was nothing left but hara-kiri, she told herself. She must plunge a sword through her worthless body like a humiliated samurai. She wondered how much it would hurt. And for how long. She wondered where to find a sword.

The watchman thrust open a carved *fusuma* screen and flung her to her knees in the room beyond. "Your pardon, Yamada-san. Forgive the intrusion, please. I have captured an intruder peering into the house."

Chiyo remained on her knees, pressing her forehead to the thickly woven tatami in the deepest bow of her life. "*Sumimasen, sumimasen,*" she said in a voice thick with shame, unable to stop saying she was sorry and using the most formal word for it, though she knew words would not help.

With disbelief, *Okaasan* said, "Chiyo?"

"No!" Denial burst from Masako as if she saw her future shattering.

"You know the intruder?" Yamada-san asked.

Otousan answered in a heavy voice that pressed Chiyo even deeper into the tatami. "*Hai*, Yamada-san. It shames me to tell you that this unworthy person is our younger daughter, Chiyo."

"Your daughter," Yamada-san repeated. "Stand please, younger sister."

It was not possible to move. Her muscles would not obey. What did it matter? Her life was over. She turned her head to the side to search the nearest wall for an ornamental sword.

Her search stopped abruptly at an astonishing display of *hina ningyo* for Hinamatsuri, the Girls' Day festival in March. The dolls, which must have belonged to Yamada-san's daughters, were traditionally arranged on a series of red-carpeted platforms, each higher than the last. At the top, the emperor and empress sat on cushions over gold-ornamented black stands.

Below them stood nobles, and below them, musicians. Tiny tables and lamps and dishes filled with small cakes, fruit-shaped candies, and sweet red beans filled the lowest tier. There was more, so much more!

It was early to set out the display. Yamada-san must have been hoping to impress Masako. The splendid, expensive dolls were handed down from daughter to daughter in families that could afford to buy them. Her shame momentarily forgotten, Chiyo strained to see into the tiny dishes.

CHAPTER 3

Again, the watchman's strong fingers grasped the back of her kimono. She gasped as he hauled her to her feet. She could not look at any of them. She should not have looked at the dolls.

"How did you come here?" asked Yamada-san.

She spoke to the floor in a whisper. "In the basket."

His voice sharpened. "I cannot hear you, younger sister. Look at me, please."

Her head felt too weighted to lift. She managed to lift her chin but not her eyes.

Yamada-san said again, "How did you come here?"

She raised her voice just enough to be heard. "I hid in the basket."

Otousan explained. "I keep a large basket tied into the cart. *Gomenasai*, Yamada-san. The fault is mine. I did not look beneath the lid before leaving home. I believed the basket to be empty."

"Ah. The only question remaining is what should be done with her."

Chiyo glanced around and felt the hand on the back of her kimono tighten. The watchman thought she might try to run away. But she was looking for a sword.

"She came here in the basket," *Otousan* said. "She will wait there for us. You have my word, Yamada-san. She will not again step onto your property."

Chiyo expected the servant to haul her out like a bag of rice, but Yamada Nori said, "I am sorry. I must disagree, Tamura-san. I will not have a child go hungry in my house while others eat."

He called another servant to set a place where Chiyo's back would be to the shoji screen and she would have to face her family instead of the glow from the stone lantern on the lawn. She would far rather have waited in the basket.

As she sank onto a cushion placed for her, she

inhaled the citrusy fragrance of yuzu and soy sauce served with an expensive baked red sea bream. It was a fish chosen to bring luck on a special day. She pushed her share around with her chopsticks. If she put one bite into her mouth, her stomach would rebel.

She risked another fleeting look down the table and noticed her sister turning quick interested glances toward their host. Masako probably thought she was keeping her expression calm, but a pink flush touched her cheeks, and when she raised her eyes, their glow told all that she was feeling.

She likes him, Chiyo realized. *She is pleased he didn't send me to wait in the basket. Masako wants to marry him and live here, even though it will mean leaving all of us.*

An hour ago, she would have been overjoyed to hear Yamada Nori say he had changed his mind and would not marry Masako. Now she realized that her wish to keep her sister at home had been selfish.

What if I ruined her chance for happiness? Chiyo heard nothing but the click of red sandalwood chopsticks against china. She felt completely alone at the table.

Belatedly, she realized that Yamada-san was

speaking to her and forced herself to listen. As if repeating his comment, he said, "You may have noticed my display of *hina ningyo*."

"*Hai*." She whispered her answer.

"You will soon see dolls of another kind. Do you know of America, a country beyond our sea?"

She nodded. They had learned about America in school.

Why was he talking to her? Hadn't she earned his disgust?

"American children," he said, "have sent more than twelve thousand dolls to the children of Japan."

Chiyo caught her breath. She could not imagine so many! They would not be *kokeshi* dolls. They might even have yellow hair. She had seen a picture of a doll with yellow hair in a book at school.

"They are called Dolls of Friendship," Yamada Nori continued. "It is said that more than two million children donated pennies to buy the dolls and send them to us."

Masako exclaimed, "Why?" and looked down swiftly after her mother's warning glance.

Yamada Nori did not seem concerned by Masako's second outburst but answered, "The hope is that friendship will develop between children of our two countries. Perhaps the dolls will prevent us from ever going to war."

"A beautiful hope," *Okaasan* said softly.

"I have heard rumblings," said *Otousan*, "talk of expanding our borders. The hope for peace may be a foolish one."

He, too, caught a look of concern from *Okaasan* and pinched a bite of sea bream in his chopsticks. "Where are those dolls now?"

"They arrived in Yokohama in mid-January."

Masako raised her head to look at her mother, probably thinking as Chiyo did that the date could mean bad fortune.

"A sad time," Yamada-san said, agreeing with their dismay. "The dolls arrived on the day Prince Chichibu returned home from England to mourn the death of our beloved Emperor Taisho. More than two thousand children greeted them for a reception held in a primary school, but they could not be welcomed with the celebration expected."

Poor dolls, Chiyo thought. *Taken away from all they have ever known and sent to a strange country, only to arrive on a sad day.*

"However, there is happier news." Yamada-san's eyes brightened. "The dolls are to enjoy a grand welcome in Tokyo during Hinamatsuri on March third. Afterward, they will be given to schools throughout Japan. One will certainly arrive at the Girls' School in Tsuchiura."

Chiyo felt as if she had missed hearing something important. Her mother and sister had been giving her glances that were by turns accusing and concerned. Now they both looked pleased. Everyone did.

What had she missed? Why was he talking about a school in distant Tsuchiura?

"As I said, the school usually accepts only the daughters of military men and high officials," Yamada-san told them, "but the headmaster is an old friend who owes me a favor. I will arrange for a place to be found for Chiyo."

They were sending her to Tsuchiura? She had never been there, but she had heard of it. The city sprawled along Lake Kasumigaura, which reached almost to the sea. This was her punishment. She would be so far from home! Would she ever see any of them again?

Yamada-san turned to her parents. "One of the young ladies there is the daughter of General Miyamoto Hiroshi. She is called Hoshi and is highly praised by her teachers for her poise and dignity. Our Chiyo will do well to become friends with Miyamoto Hoshi and follow her example."

He studied Chiyo while her face grew warm and she put down the piece of preserved peach she had picked up with her fingers. "She will learn proper behavior in the school and put her hill country wildness behind her."

Chiyo picked up chopsticks, her fingertips whitening with her tight hold. The school might be better than hara-kiri, she told herself, but not by much. In a near whisper, she asked *Otousan*, "When will I be sent to that place?"

She didn't dare ask how long she must stay away from her home and everyone she loved. She was pretty sure she knew what he would say: *You must stay away until you learn to behave like Miyamoto Hoshi.* Already, she could not like the girl.

CHAPTER 4

Yamada-san has business in Tsuchiura," *Otousan* explained during the long ride home from the *omiai*. "In three days, he will take you to the new school in his buggy."

Chiyo watched the lantern sway with the steps of the ox. Beyond, a full moon rose over the mountains. How could she admire the moon? In three days, she must leave her family and travel many miles down the mountain, a full day's ride in a horse-drawn buggy. She was to leave her family.

Probably forever!

On the third morning, well before the sun was up, Chiyo stood silently while her mother fastened bundled belongings to her back, along with a cushion for the floor of the new classroom.

"*Otousan* cannot spare more time from the fields," her mother had warned the night before. "You must walk, as your sister did each day when she worked in Yamada-san's rice paddies."

Okaasan's dark eyes had filled with concern. "We know you will make us proud of you, Chiyo-chan. Observe well the girl who is so respected by her teachers."

Miyamoto Hoshi. The name was burned across Chiyo's mind. That girl was apparently the most perfectly behaved in all of Japan. What could she say to someone like that?

Yesterday, her last day in the village school, her friend Yumi had hugged her good-bye. "Come back and tell us all about it!"

Chiyo's fears leaped to her tongue. "What can I say to the daughters of important men? Do you think they are interested in how the rice grows on our small farm or where to find wild herbs?"

"They should be," Yumi answered loyally. "You have something better than their fathers' importance. You have a loving family. And true friends. That's worth talking about."

Chiyo knew that her family and friends loved

her. Since the disaster of the *omiai*, everyone had treated her so gently, she felt even worse. Now, as her family prepared to send her away, *Okaasan* spoke more intensely than was usual for her. "Japan is changing, Chiyo-chan. You must be brave and fierce while learning to change with it. The new school offers you that. Put fear behind and seize this opportunity."

Her sister clasped both her hands. "Do your very best, little sister, so Yamada-san will bring you from the school for my wedding in May."

A hollow feeling had been building inside Chiyo since she learned of the school in Tsuchiura. Now that hollow began to fill with tears. "I promise to watch Miss Miyamoto," she said. "I will be like her . . . and I will come home. . . ."

She couldn't say more. The next sound would be a sob.

"It is time to leave," their mother warned. "Yamada-san will start for Tsuchiura at dawn, and his home is a long walk from our door."

Chiyo clung to her mother and then her sister, their hugs made awkward by the bundle on her back. When she left her warmly lit doorway and made her way to the dark mountain path, she longed to rush back to her family.

Miyamoto Hoshi, the daughter of a high-ranking military man, would not show fear. Neither would Chiyo, the daughter of an ordinary farmer. Keeping her spine straight and her fears hidden, she began the five-mile foot journey down the mountain.

She pulled Masako's *kokeshi* from a fold of her kimono and held Momo tightly, drawing comfort from her sister's love.

Boulders and small waterfalls and leaning trees made splashes of white or darker shadows. Though the distance was long, the path led downhill and vanished more quickly beneath her steps than she had thought possible. The need to restore her honor to her family kept her hurrying forward.

She shivered despite her heavy cotton kimono. Walking would soon warm her, although fallen snow still lay along the roadsides. She was used to being out before dawn, but always in the bustle of a busy family. Now, as tree branches threw darker shadows wriggling across the road, she tried to step over them, half-fearing they would grab her ankles.

"It's good I am almost grown," she told the shadows. "I'm not easily scared like Yumi's little sister." And as the day began to lighten, there was Yamada Nori's gate standing open for her. She rushed across gleaming stepping-stones to knock on the door.

A maid directed her to a room where she might refresh herself. When she returned, another maid pointed the way through a side door where Yamada Nori watched a servant harness his beautiful horse to a light buggy with a bench seat.

When he nodded to her, she bowed swiftly and hurried to join him. The servant placed her bundle and cushion in the back as Yamada-san lifted her onto the seat. Chiyo clutched the side. This was not like the oxcart. This was much farther from the ground. The horse didn't stand still like the patient ox, but shifted its feet, making the buggy tremble.

Yamada-san clicked his tongue. The carriage jolted ahead, feeling even more fragile when it moved forward at a fast trot. What if they overturned on the uneven road?

Again, she held tightly to Momo. Somehow, the buggy stayed upright and they continued down the mountain.

Time became measured by the changing scene. The sun rose higher over the fast narrow stream that churned past her village. The stream gained strength from small waterfalls and side streams as they traveled lower, until finally it became a river. As the sun moved toward the west, the river spread into the long lake called Kasumigaura, its blue waters gleaming in the late-winter light. The very long ride was finally over.

They traveled through streets that seemed to exist in a different world than the one Chiyo knew, one even larger and busier than she had expected. Yamada-san halted the horse beside a roofed gate with a plant-lined bamboo fence to either side. Freshly washed stepping-stones led across a landscaped yard to a long building where doorways opened onto an outside walkway. A series of tiled roofs rose one over another. She could see the roof of a taller building beyond and thought there must be a courtyard in the center.

The fresh green scent of plants she didn't recognize made her feel even farther from home. She swallowed hard, feeling as if the koi from ponds beyond the gate swam within her, nervously fluttering their fins.

For the first time since a brief stop for a box lunch provided by his housekeeper, Yamada-san turned and spoke. "The day grows late. I must go on.

Introduce yourself to Hanarai-sensei. He is in charge of the school and is expecting you."

The koi Chiyo imagined inside her stomach swam even faster. She was to enter this strange place without even Yamada-san to help her find her way.

CHAPTER 5

She tried to think. What would Miyamoto Hoshi do? That perfect girl would keep her face serene, Chiyo decided. Then she would ask someone where to find the headmaster.

Yamada-san had not finished talking. "If you receive a good report from the school's staff at the end of April, you may return home for your sister's wedding in May. If not, you will stay here and work harder to improve."

"I must go home for Masako's wedding," Chiyo exclaimed. "I promised."

Yamada-san's eyes narrowed. "I would not expect to hear such an outburst from a student at this school."

Chiyo followed his glance toward a group of girls in a doorway, some in kimonos, others wearing dark skirts and blouses. All of them hurried along the walkway to another door. Her clothes were nothing like theirs, and despite Yamada-san's warning, Chiyo said, "They may not like me."

"Liking is not important." He climbed from the carriage and came around to lift her to the street. "You are here to learn. That is important. That is all that is important. Do you understand?"

He was right. Bowing, she answered softly, "*Hai,* Yamada-san. I will work hard."

He indicated three girls in kimonos talking outside one of the rooms. "The taller girl on the right is Miyamoto Hoshi. Honor her with close attention. Shape your behavior after hers."

Chiyo studied the fashionable girl who even from this distance looked frighteningly different. Forcing doubts aside, she told herself she could not miss her sister's wedding. Bowing, she murmured, "*Hai,* Yamada-san."

"Good." He removed her bundle and floor cushion from the back, then handed her a small purse of red silk weighted with coins. "Go now."

"*Arigatogozaimasu,*" she said, thanking him in surprise for his generosity. In her family, every sen had to be spent carefully. She had never before had even one of her own.

Yamada Nori had scarcely spoken to her. He was leaving her alone outside this strange school. His buggy wheels rolled smoothly away, sounding as different from the squeaking wheels of her father's oxcart as he was from her father.

But Yamada-san and his horse were her last ties to home, and he had given her money so she would have some independence. For one painful moment as the carriage rolled away, she struggled not to run after him.

Her destiny was set. She could not change it. Holding her belongings as if cradling part of home to her heart, she walked slowly over the gleaming stepping-stones.

The nearer she came to the girls in heavy silk kimonos, the more country dressed she felt, but Chiyo studied their expressions and arranged her own face into as near a copy as she could manage without a mirror. The three girls looked as if nothing had ever disturbed the calm of their lives and nothing ever would.

Was it true? Did they live charmed lives? Or was an expression as smooth as a flowing stream part of the new way she must learn?

None of them wore their hair hanging loose, as the girls her age did at home. Two wore paper ribbons to tie up the long shining lengths. Miyamoto Hoshi wore hers in a braid. They could not be ready to graduate from elementary school for at least another year. Yet to Chiyo, they all looked ready to wear their hair in the round buns meant to represent buds about to bloom into young women.

They're girls, Chiyo reassured herself, *just girls like me.* She would start by saying good afternoon, and she would remember to say please.

Still trying to mirror their expressions, she walked to Miyamoto Hoshi and bowed politely. "*Konnichiwa,* I am Tamura Chiyo, a new student. Would you please direct me to the headmaster?"

The other two girls looked at Hoshi. Hoshi's perfect expression changed very little, yet the shape of her eyebrows, the turn of her lips, however subtle, suggested a lady regarding a peasant.

"Another foreign *ningyo,*" she said to her friends, who giggled. To Chiyo, she said, "You have confused our school with your own. I suggest you consult a member of the staff for directions." The three of them hurried away with the quick small steps required by their kimonos.

Chiyo looked after them, puzzled. Had Yamada

Nori made a mistake? Of course not. He was a friend of the headmaster here. And he had recognized Miyamoto Hoshi. Why did the girl call her a foreign doll?

We have not been introduced, she reminded herself, pushing back a stir of resistance. *Girls here live by different rules. The difference is what I have come here to learn. That I feel snubbed is a lesson, not an insult.*

Another girl came onto the walkway, one who looked a great deal friendlier.

"I am Nakata Hana," the girl said. "Welcome to Tsuchiura, Tamura Chiyo. Now that you've met the worst of us, you must meet the best. That's me!"

Chiyo liked Hana's smile and the sparkle in her eyes, but she couldn't get past Hoshi's odd comment. "She called me *ningyo.* Why would she call me a doll?"

"I'll carry your bundle to the sleeping room," Hana said, taking it from Chiyo. "Go through that door and along the inner courtyard to Headmaster Hanarai's office." She paused before adding, "Don't let Hoshi bother you."

"But *ningyo?*"

Hana lowered her voice. "She was referring to

thousands of American Friendship Dolls that have arrived in Yokohama. Her father is a general who says the dolls are an attempt to buy our goodwill, so she calls them unwanted foreign dolls."

Chiyo was startled to hear that anyone disapproved of the dolls Yamada Nori had described with enthusiasm during the *omiai*. Hoshi's comment troubled her even more. "I am not foreign."

Hana laughed. "To Hoshi, anyone who is not from Tokyo or Tsuchiura is foreign and therefore unwelcome."

Chiyo could not return the smile. A single thought burned through her. *I'm to model myself after Miyamoto Hoshi and I am not sure I can like her.*

"I have changed my mind," Hana said. "I will walk with you to the headmaster. You should not have to go there alone." She looked curiously at Chiyo. "Why are you alone? Did you fall from the sky?"

Chiyo heard the joke but still could not smile. "Yamada Nori-san, the man my sister will marry, brought me in his carriage. But he had business in town and couldn't wait."

Did that sound as if she had been dumped at the

gate? "He is wealthy," she said, trying to explain. "Very busy."

"Is your father in the military?" Hana asked, making Chiyo wonder if the girl's offer to walk to the office was based on curiosity. "Or is he in politics, like mine?"

"My father is a farmer in a village in the mountains."

Hana said in surprise, "He can afford to send you here?" She added with quick apology, "*Gomen, gomen!* You have said your sister's husband-to-be is wealthy. All that matters is that you are here."

Her smile looked as if she meant it, and Chiyo tried not to feel offended as Hana led her along an inner walkway beside a courtyard. She remembered telling Yumi she would not fit in and feared even more that it was true. The tranquil flow of water in a nearby fountain failed to calm the imaginary koi now swimming frantically inside her stomach.

"These are the classrooms," Hana said, motioning toward the building facing the street. She swept her hand toward a second building on the far side of the courtyard. "There are more classrooms. The dining hall is in the taller building to our right, with the sleeping area above it." Having given information, she turned to Chiyo with curiosity in her eyes. "Does your father have a very large farm?"

For a brief moment, Chiyo wanted to answer yes, that he had an estate with many men to work on it. She wanted to pretend she belonged with these girls. Fiercely, she told herself that she did belong. Her way was paid and she was one of them. "Our farm is small. Yamada-san arranged for me to come here."

She drew a deep breath and challenged Hana with the truth. If Hana wanted to end the friendship before it could begin, she could do so. "I am here to model myself after Miyamoto Hoshi."

Hana clapped one hand over her mouth, then lowered it to demand, "Who wants you to be like Hoshi?"

"Yamada Nori-san."

"Why? He is not marrying you!"

"No," Chiyo agreed. "But he is marrying into my family. I am here to learn to behave properly." She drew her mouth into the rosebud shape she had seen on Miyamoto Hoshi.

Hana looked as if she were trying to decide whether to laugh or scowl. "Does he know Miyamoto Hoshi?"

"He knows of her."

Hana shook her head. "Hoshi has pretty manners while speaking to adults. If you cross words with her, you will find she is as tough as a clay pot." The sparkle returned to Hana's eyes. "Of course, she thinks she is fine china."

"Still, I, too, must appear to be fine china." Chiyo struggled to make her expression serene.

Hana crossed her arms over Chiyo's bundle. "I think you are no more fine china than I am. What did you do to make anyone want you to change?"

Chiyo hesitated, hoping Hana would not carry her words to all the girls in the school. "Um, I sneaked into my sister's *omiai*."

A delighted shriek burst from Hana. "I like you, Tamura Chiyo! Inside, you are strong. You might even push Hoshi from the pedestal she has built for herself."

"Push her off!" Chiyo exclaimed. "I'm supposed to be like her! I must be or I cannot go home to Masako's wedding." She clasped one hand over the *kokeshi* tucked into her kimono as she added, "I must be there!"

"You will never be like Hoshi." Hana shifted Chiyo's bundle under one arm and clasped Chiyo's hand. "That is a good thing, for even Hoshi should not be like Hoshi."

She tugged Chiyo forward. "You and I are going to be great friends! And there . . ." She motioned toward a door at the end of the walkway. "There is Hanarai-sensei's office."

CHAPTER 6

With the imaginary koi leaping inside her, Chiyo followed Hana to an office at the far side of the classrooms.

Inside, she bowed politely with Hana, glimpsing Hanarai-sensei through her eyelashes. He was a large man, a door she could not pass unless he wished it.

He studied her without smiling. "You are the girl whom Yamada Nori wishes to enroll."

For a frantic moment, Chiyo thought he was closing the door against her, that his large square body would block her from the school. If she wasn't accepted here, what would she do? Where would she go?

Softly, she said, "I have promised to work very hard, Hanarai-sensei."

"We shall see." He turned to Hana. "Miss Nakata, please take our new student to Mrs. Ogata. See that a uniform is found for her."

Relief swept through Chiyo. He was letting her stay even though he looked at her as if examining a species of moth he did not wish to add to his collection of butterflies.

She pictured a scale with saucers on each side. One side weighed a good report for Yamada-san. The other side weighed bad reports. She hoped that second side would remain empty, but she could see it was going to take work from her before Headmaster sent a report to the good side.

"*Arigatogozaimasu,*" she said, bowing again before following Hana from the office. Relief made the air of the courtyard feel fresher. The scent of unfamiliar flowers smelled sweeter. Silently, Chiyo promised that Headmaster would not regret enrolling her.

"This way," Hana said, leading her along a pathway to the building she had pointed out earlier. Inside, stairs at one end led to a large open room. Mrs. Ogata, a sturdy woman with a crisp manner, also looked at Chiyo as if she saw a moth.

While Hana hurried away to class, the woman led Chiyo to a closet with a sliding panel. Under Mrs. Ogata's sharp eye, Chiyo arranged her floor cushion and few belongings on a shelf below the rolled futon that would be hers.

As if reading from a list she no longer needed, Mrs. Ogata explained the rules. "To pay for their stay, boarding girls are expected to rise before daylight and begin their chores. Those will include cleaning not only your own space, but the walls and floors. You will also help with laundry, carry in bathwater, and wash dishes after meals."

That sounded like a lot to do in addition to schoolwork, but Chiyo was used to rising early and working hard. She was glad she would be busy. She would have less time to miss her family.

As she followed Mrs. Ogata back down the stairs, the courtyard filled with the sounds of girls' voices and clattering *geta*. Classes had ended for the day. Chiyo glimpsed the town girls on their way home, several wearing heavy silk kimonos. Talking and laughing together, they made their way down the walkways and out of the gates, clearly the butterflies in Hanarai-sensei's collection. He could be proud of them. Could he be proud of a moth? *Yes,*

Chiyo told herself, *for moths are strong and beautiful in their own way.*

In the dining area, Hana called her to a space near the end of a long table. Chiyo joined her, glancing around the table. Miyamoto Hoshi was not here, but she could learn from these girls. A delicious aroma rose as a small baked fish was set before her. The moment she began to eat, Mrs. Ogata interrupted. "Miss Tamura, take smaller bites, please. You will never see Miyamoto Hoshi shove an entire fish into her mouth."

Country girls learned to eat fast so they could be in the fields before dawn and do as much work as possible before school. Chiyo felt her appetite disappear beneath a rush of embarrassment.

"You'll get used to her," Hana promised.

Mrs. Ogata exclaimed, "Miss Nakata, Miyamoto Hoshi will never show food in her mouth when she speaks."

A girl nearby said, "I wonder if we will ever learn manners as perfect as Hoshi's."

Hana covered her mouth with her hand while her eyes sparkled. Chiyo could not smile back. Again, she felt out of place.

Hana may laugh, but I will hold my mouth as

Hoshi does and eat slowly and learn to walk with quick, tiny steps. When Yamada-san returns, he will be proud of a new Chiyo.

As she carefully separated a small piece of fish with her chopsticks, the effort felt stiff and wrong. Obviously, there was more to learn at Girls' School than writing kanji characters and learning dance steps.

By the time she relaxed on her futon, Chiyo was happy to have become friends with Hana. She thought the school's strict policies could never dim Hana's laughter.

"We are learning a song for the American dolls," Hana said from the next sleeping mat. "It's called 'The Welcome Song.' Do you know it?"

"No, but I'd like to," Chiyo said, remembering the dolls Yamada Nori had described.

"I'll teach you," Hana assured her. "It begins like this. . . ."

But Mrs. Ogata called for silence and put out the light.

Chiyo turned restlessly. Even the sounds were wrong. She listened for frogs but instead heard occasional footsteps and voices from the street that made her feel unsafe.

She reached into her folded clothing and

brought out the *kokeshi* doll her sister had given her. Holding Momo close, smoothing her thumb along the doll's painted kimono, she thought of home until gradually sleep claimed her.

After chores and breakfast, Chiyo walked to class with Hana and several others. Each carried a cushion, so Chiyo was surprised to see desks and chairs in the classroom. "Why are we bringing cushions?"

"They make the chairs more comfortable," Hana said with a grin. "And we use them to save a good seat in the room before the town girls take them all."

Another girl called and Hana went away to talk to her. Chiyo decided on a seat at the front of the room where she could see and hear the teacher. Yamada-san would not be sorry that he was spending so much money to send her to this school.

She placed her cushion on a seat in the front row, then joined another girl who was sharpening her slate pencil at a table in a corner. Raised voices told her that the town girls were arriving for class. As they came in, their confidence took over the room. Most wore school uniforms today, but even in dark skirts and blouses, they dressed more richly than Chiyo in her borrowed uniform.

A question asked in a pleasant voice with a bite beneath it silenced everyone. "Whose cushion is this?"

Before she turned, Chiyo knew the cushion would be hers and that Miyamoto Hoshi would be holding it by one corner as if it were a fish going bad. *I will remember and copy the patience with which she observes the unwanted item.*

On the heels of that thought came another, hotter one. *No one told me others might have saved seats ahead of time.* She drew in a breath to answer. "The cushion is mine."

The stylish town girl looked at her with pity on her perfect face. "You are new, so you do not know you have broken a rule. My name is Miyamoto Hoshi. I sit in this chair. Every day."

Instead of offering the cushion to Chiyo, she handed it to a girl in the row behind. That girl threw it to a girl in the next row. While Chiyo watched, her face growing hotter, the cushion flew from girl to girl toward the back of the room. Some girls hid smirks, while others looked sympathetic. No one looked surprised.

Across the room, Hana pursed her mouth in the "Hoshi shape" Chiyo had worn when trying to be like Hoshi the day before. Chiyo understood the warning to remain serene. She thought that holding their mouths like rosebuds might quickly become a joke between Hana and herself.

But she didn't feel like laughing or even smiling. Humiliated and confused, she stood frozen at the front of the room while her cushion sailed from girl to girl.

CHAPTER 7

The sensei, Mrs. Kaito, swept into the room and cast a sharp glance over them all. The cushion landed abruptly on the floor at one side. Sensei motioned toward it. "Whose property is this?"

I should have asked where to sit before placing my cushion on a chair, Chiyo told herself. Feeling her skin grow hot, she said with apology, "*Sumimasen*, Sensei, the cushion is mine."

"You will retrieve it, please." The teacher turned to Hoshi. "Miss Tamura has come to us from a country school and will need to catch up with the rest of you. I wish her to sit at the front.

Since you are an excellent student, Miss Miyamoto, you will not mind moving to a seat at the back for a time."

Hoshi's expression remained as untroubled as a still pool. She flowed to her feet, placed her hands at her waist, and bowed gracefully, first to the teacher, then to Chiyo. When she moved to the rear, she seemed to float rather than walk in the kimono she preferred to wear.

Hoshi acted older than the rest, Chiyo thought. How did she walk as she did, as if a stream carried her instead of her two feet? If she felt annoyed to be told to sit at the back, her face did not show it.

It was too late to return her unexpected bow. Belatedly, Chiyo, too, bowed to the sensei. As she did, Masako's *kokeshi* clattered to the floor from the pocket of her borrowed shirt. Girls giggled while she snatched it up.

"What is that, Miss Tamura?" Sensei asked.

Chiyo held out the doll. "My sister gave it to me to remind me of home."

"Place it on my desk, please."

Everyone seemed to hold their breath, waiting to see what she would do. For a rebellious moment, Chiyo thought of shoving Momo into her pocket.

As if the doll spoke with her sister's voice, she

imagined Masako saying, *Stay calm and make us proud of you.*

She could do that. She would do that. Softly, she said, "*Hai*, Sensei," and placed the doll on a corner of the desk before retrieving her cushion and returning to the chair at the front.

She wondered if Sensei had asked her to sit there in order to keep an eye on a possible troublemaker. The thought brought new heat to her face.

The teacher displayed the doll to the class. "*Kokeshi* are made by craftsmen in Northern Japan. Each is signed on its base." She turned the doll, showing the artist's kanji signature at the bottom. "As all of you know, dolls have long held an important place in our culture."

She placed Momo on her desk. "You also know of the American Friendship Dolls now in Yokohama."

In the back, Hoshi must have raised her hand. The teacher said, "Miss Miyamoto? Does General Miyamoto welcome this gesture of friendship?"

Hoshi spoke with a mixture of sorrow and iron in her voice. "My father says our country must expand our borders, not hold our hands out for dolls like children offered sweets. If expansion requires war, then war will come. Friendship Dolls will not prevent it."

Everyone had turned in their seats to look at her. Now they swiveled back for the teacher's response.

"Thank you, Miss Miyamoto," Sensei said. "Your honorable father is highly respected, but I feel I must point out that none of us can see the future."

"Father says America is a weak, frightened country to send dolls to us," Hoshi answered. "I am sorry, but I cannot welcome them."

"Our emperor has welcomed the dolls," the teacher reminded her quietly. "During a ceremony to be held in Tokyo, the granddaughter of the shogun Prince Tokugawa will accept the first doll. I believe the exchange will be charming."

"May it go well," Hoshi said, adding sadly, "My father says Japanese children must show they cannot be bought with pretty dolls." She bowed her head, but not before Chiyo saw a surprisingly unpleasant glitter in her eyes. That glitter said that Miyamoto Hoshi agreed with her father.

Kaito-sensei rang a small bell on her desk, calling for order as several of the girls spoke at once.

"While I greatly respect General Miyamoto," she said when they were quiet again, "in this case I must agree with our emperor and empress, who are welcoming the dolls."

Chiyo stared at Masako's *kokeshi* on a corner of the teacher's desk while trying to understand Miyamoto Hoshi. Of course the girl must respect her father's views.

"We are told that the American children donated pennies for the project," Sensei continued. "Our emperor will express our country's gratitude. You—all of you—are invited to help pay for dolls to be made by our finest doll makers and sent in return to the children of America."

Chiyo sat straighter on her cushion, thinking of the coins that Yamada Nori had given her. "I would like to donate a sen."

"*Arigatogozaimasu*, Miss Tamura. I will place a donation box on my desk."

Chiyo waited to hear Hoshi offer to donate a sen, or even several, but the girl remained silent. Maybe she felt insulted by the teacher's failure to agree with her father.

Sensei continued, "The *Torei Ningyo*, or, in English, Dolls of Return Gratitude, will be ninety centimeters in height—thirty-five inches—the size of a small child."

Again, a murmur moved about the classroom. Chiyo thought of Yumi's three-year-old sister. She was about ninety centimeters tall. The dolls going to America would be the size of little Kimi. Yamada-san had described the American dolls as much smaller, small enough to carry about in her arms.

"Japan will send fifty-eight beautiful *Torei Ningyo* to America," Sensei added. "Who can tell me why that number was selected?"

The girls looked at one another. No one raised a hand. Maybe they were afraid to give a wrong answer. At last, Kimiko, a girl next to Chiyo, said, "It cannot be for the number of prefectures in Japan. There are only forty-seven."

Another girl risked asking, "Will they be named for our cities?"

"You are both correct," Sensei answered, and a soft sigh of relief swept the class. "Most of the fifty-eight will represent our prefectures. Others will bear the names of territories and of our largest cities."

She glanced around the class. "Can you tell

me what the fifty-eighth doll is to represent?" She glanced toward the back. "Miss Miyamoto?"

"I am sorry, Sensei," Hoshi answered. "I do not know."

Chiyo saw several girls glance at one another. Was Hoshi sulking and refusing to answer? Then a girl near Kimiko suggested, "The emperor and empress."

"You are close," the teacher told her.

Chiyo raised her hand as inspiration struck. "Will the last doll represent all of Japan?"

"*Hai*," Sensei said. "The finest doll will be given by the emperor and empress and will be called Miss Dai Nippon, or, in English, 'Miss Japan.'"

Sensei marked a mathematics problem on the board, explaining the distance from San Francisco to Yokohama and telling them that the American dolls' journey had taken ten days.

"Use your slates to work out answers. How fast did the ships travel? How far did they travel in one day?"

Chiyo tried to work out the problems, but her thoughts kept drifting from the ships to the dolls they had carried. What would they look like? Some might have blond curly hair and even blue eyes, far different from dolls made in Japan.

She hoped she would have a chance to hold one of them.

"Miss Tamura." Sensei's voice wrenched her back to the classroom. "Do you have the answer?"

"No, Sensei," she answered, regretting the seat in the front row. "I am still working on it."

Hoshi spoke into the pause, again sounding sad. "Be careful of opening your hearts to the dolls, my friends. My father, General Miyamoto, would give his life for our emperor, but he fears that someday we will regret welcoming these foreign dolls. They should be destroyed. The emperor will come to see that."

The other girls murmured in dismay, and for a moment, Chiyo felt sorry for Hoshi. What must it be like to have a father who wanted the emperor to wage war against dolls?

When class was dismissed, the girls left the room in orderly rows to go down the walkway to dance class. Chiyo looked wistfully at Masako's *kokeshi*. She didn't dare step out of line to take it, and reminded herself that Momo was safe on Sensei's desk. She would come back for the doll at lunchtime.

CHAPTER 8

The other girls in dance class moved like reeds on a pond, in graceful steps familiar to them but not to Chiyo. Yet the music flowed through her as it did when she sang with the wind while following paths through the hills near her home.

"*Sumimasen*," she said in apology to Oki-sensei, the dance teacher. "I have never learned this dance. It isn't taught in my other school."

"Just follow the steps of the girl in front." The teacher guided her into line and hurried across the room to correct another group.

The girl in front was Hoshi. She seemed unaware of Chiyo behind her. Hoping she wouldn't turn around, Chiyo concentrated on copying her steps.

Hoshi's foot moved sharply.

Chiyo followed. Too late, she saw Hoshi pull her own step back. It was a trick.

The teacher hurried to straighten the line. "I'm afraid you are far behind the others, Miss Tamura. Please sit on the side. Watch how the others move."

Chiyo found a seat beneath a window, telling herself, *I should have pulled my step back when Hoshi moved sharply. Everyone behind me became confused.*

It was not entirely my fault! Inside her head, resentment spoke louder as the lesson began again. In her mind, she removed dance class from the bad side of the scale where it had landed. The general's daughter had deliberately made a false step. *That should not weigh against me.*

During a break near the end of the session, Hana slipped onto the seat next to her. "It's too bad you don't sing. That could put Hoshi in her place."

Chiyo looked at her, startled. "I do sing. I like to."

"Are you good?"

"They said so at my other school. What does that have to do with Hoshi?"

"Nothing. I should not have mentioned it." Hana slumped forward, one hand on her chin. "The vocal group is filled, with Hoshi singing the lead. She always sings the lead."

"I'm not surprised."

"She's good," Hana said, "but not as good as the teachers say. They rave over her because her father is important. And . . . his wealthy family gives a lot of money to the school."

Can I sing better than the girl the teachers favor? As pleasant as it would be to outshine Hoshi, Chiyo longed to join the vocal group for another reason. There, she would be judged by her ability, not by her family's lack of wealth. But Hana had said the vocal group was filled.

She realized that all the other girls were surging to their feet and bowing. As she rose with them, Chiyo saw that Headmaster Hanarai had come into the room.

"Why is he here?" Hana whispered. "He never comes in." Oki-sensei's assistant strummed her koto, and all the girls were told to resume their dance. "*Everyone*, please, Miss Tamura."

Everyone? This was the one time she wanted to sit out a dance! She concentrated hard, trying to sway like a reed but feeling more like a stick. Headmaster spoke to the teacher, then looked directly at Chiyo with his mouth turned down.

Her heart sank. *They're talking about me. Maybe Yamada-san has asked for a report.* Her knees felt weak, and as the others swayed to the left, she jerked to the right.

"Miss Tamura," Sensei called. "Come to my desk, please."

Chiyo felt Hana's encouraging touch on her arm, while down the room pitying murmurs could only have come from Hoshi.

Chiyo's feet felt even more leaden than when she had missed the dance step. The smooth wood floor clutched her as if she trudged through mud. Headmaster Hanarai's troubled expression drove her gaze downward. His voice was as troubled as his face. "You are not doing well with dance."

Chiyo told the floor softly, "I am trying to learn."

"Yes, well. It cannot be easy to join a more advanced class in the middle of the session." He added to the teacher as if Chiyo no longer stood listening, "I will be sorry to disappoint my old friend Yamada Nori. He had hopes for the girl."

Chiyo wanted to say, *I had hopes for the school!* She swallowed the words. She could almost hear *Okaasan* warning, *A worthy woman is never sarcastic.*

Must a worthy woman remain silent while told she is nothing? Should she be quiet while her chance to attend her sister's wedding vanished? *All Hoshi has done has only made me stronger.*

Although she had not been invited to speak, Chiyo said, "I am sorry the school has no singing group. My teachers have said my voice is good."

Headmaster Hanarai's expression lightened. "You sing? As a matter of fact, Miss Tamura, we do have a vocal group. The group is filled, but perhaps an exception can be made. Come with me. We will speak to Watanabe-sensei at once."

Even a small victory over Hoshi felt good, but beneath it, Chiyo worried. Maybe she should not have spoken. The dances were all unfamiliar. Songs here might also be different than the ones her old classmates and family enjoyed.

Only the teacher was in the music room when she reached it with Headmaster Hanarai. A slender man with a small pointed beard and intense eyes, Watanabe-sensei sat on a floor cushion fingering a koto and making notes on a music sheet. He rose at once to bow to the headmaster. While Chiyo waited just inside the doorway, the two argued at length. It was clear that Watanabe-sensei did not wish to add even one more voice.

At last, with a resigned expression, Sensei motioned her forward. "Very well, Miss Tamura. I will hear you sing, but I make no promises." He aimed the last comment at Headmaster Hanarai.

"Do not disappoint us," the headmaster warned as Chiyo stood beside the koto, her hands folded at her waist. When Watanabe-sensei indicated that she should sing, Chiyo did not think of Hoshi's muffled laughter. Her heart and mind filled with the natural music of home so that she was barely aware of the koto following her lead.

She sent her voice soaring with the wind as it danced through canyons, rippling the leaves of trees, challenging birds as they dared fly against it, and at last rising again to the sky. She put her heart and love for home into her song while the classroom fell away. When the music students arrived and quietly took their places, she scarcely heard or saw them. She was alone in the mountains she loved.

The song ended. The koto's last notes became the fading wind. Then it, too, fell silent.

For a long moment, no one made a sound. Chiyo couldn't look at the class. *It was all wrong,* she told herself. *They are from the city. I should have thought of city sounds. But I don't know them yet.*

CHAPTER 9

Headmaster Hanarai broke the silence. "Is she good enough for the Tsuchiura Girls' School chorus?" Amusement sounded in his voice as he looked from the music teacher to the girls who had come in so silently.

Approval hummed through Watanabe-sensei's voice. "Raw but trainable, with exceptional purity."

Turning to the class, the music teacher asked, "Did you hear the notes in her upper register? They were as fluid as birdsong. That is what I have been trying to teach you." He turned back to Headmaster Hanarai. "I welcome the chance to work with this girl."

"Miss Miyamoto," Headmaster Hanarai warned with a light in his eyes that made Chiyo wonder if he appreciated Hoshi as much as was thought. "You may be in danger of losing your position of first voice in our vocal group."

Hoshi didn't answer. She was perfectly still. *The way a snake is still,* Chiyo thought, *until it strikes.*

Even so, pleasure made her steps light. Sensei had liked her singing. So had the headmaster. She felt sure they would give good reports of her to Yamada-san.

She wasn't as certain when Watanabe-sensei kept her after class to test her on the welcome song for the dolls everyone was learning. "You have an excellent voice," he told her, "but you have a great amount to learn."

"I'll help." Hana, who had waited in the doorway, came forward to stand beside Chiyo. "I know the welcome song and will be happy to teach it to Chiyo."

"Very good." Watanabe-sensei closed his lesson book. "Welcome to the vocal group, Miss Tamura."

Moments later, as Chiyo and Hana cut across the

courtyard toward the dining hall, Hana frowned. "Where is she going?"

Chiyo saw Hoshi hurrying along the far walkway and wondered why Hana had pointed her out.

"Hoshi always eats lunch with her friends near the koi pond in front," Hana explained. "She's going the wrong way." Giggling, she added, "Maybe she is going off to sulk now that you are Watanabe-sensei's new favorite."

"Not favorite," Chiyo protested quickly. "Just new." But pleasure wouldn't be buried under modesty. Watanabe-sensei heard many voices. That he liked her singing gave her a burst of confidence, and the good side of her imaginary scale gained weight.

"She deliberately tricked you into a misstep in dance," Hana exclaimed.

Chiyo hesitated. "It may have been an accident."

"Chiyo! Don't make excuses for the general's daughter. You're thinking like a peasant observing a landowner. That's how she wants you to think. She's wrong. You are as good as she is. Better! Remember that!"

Trying to keep her expression sober, Chiyo

tucked her hands at her waist and bowed, teasing Hana while agreeing with her.

Kaito-sensei's classroom was just ahead, and with a jolt of conscience, Chiyo remembered her sister's doll. "Hana, I need to get Momo. I'll meet you in the dining hall."

"I'll find seats together," Hana agreed, while Chiyo hurried to the empty classroom. How different it felt with no students inside, as if the room expanded in their absence. Her steps echoed when she crossed to Sensei's desk.

Masako's doll was not there.

Chiyo stared at the empty space, trying to see a doll where there was none. Momo had to be here! She lifted a paper, then shifted a book. Maybe the teacher had put the doll away. Did she dare open a drawer?

As she hesitated, Kaito-sensei said from the doorway, "Miss Tamura. What are you doing?"

"I'm looking for my doll." A chill ran through her, carrying an awful truth. "It isn't here."

"I left it on the desk," Sensei said. "One of your friends must have taken it for you. Ask them."

The chill Chiyo felt inside spread to the ends of her fingers. Only one girl might have taken the *kokeshi*, one who didn't want a country girl in the school and meant to make her miserable.

"*Sumimasen*," she murmured, asking the teacher's pardon for rushing from the room.

Hoshi was no longer in sight. Chiyo looked one way, then the other, the sense of dread urging her to hurry. She ran through the school and out to the koi pond in front, where several girls sat on a stone bench with their *bento* box lunches. "Have you seen Hoshi?"

They shook their heads. "She isn't here."

One of the girls looked toward the school roof. "Is that smoke?"

"Just the gardener burning trash," another answered.

Chiyo's heart leaped into her throat. "Where? Behind the buildings? How does he get there?"

The first girl shrugged. "There's a gate where the walkway meets the far corner of the building."

Where Hoshi was headed!

"*Arigato!*" She threw the thank-you over her shoulder as she ran into the school and across the courtyard. She wrenched open the gate.

At the back of the yard, a gardener tended a

small pile of burning trash. Chiyo rushed to the pile and grabbed for the ends of dead branches.

"Miss!" the gardener exclaimed. "You'll be burned!"

"My doll! A girl threw my doll in!"

"Come away. Let me see." He kicked the fire apart, scattering burning branches.

Chiyo saw the little *kokeshi* in the coals and lunged forward, but the gardener caught her arm and pulled her back. "Stop! It's hot!"

"Momo!" Chiyo shouted. "She's right there!"

"I see her." He swung his rake forward. In the same moment, the fire flared. Flames licked over the doll, hungry and orange.

"No!" Chiyo screamed.

The gardener raked the burning doll from the fire. He caught the *kokeshi* into his gloved hands and closed them. When he opened his hands again, the flames were extinguished, but the doll's head was badly charred. Only her sweet smile remained.

"I'm sorry, miss," the gardener said gently. "She can't be saved. Shall I put her back in?"

Chiyo gasped, and he added quickly, "Or I can dig a nice little grave . . . near the small shrine there. Would you like that?"

"No." She gasped for air enough to force words past anger and anguish. "I'm going to keep her."

The gardener looked troubled, but he let her take the doll from his glove.

She cradled Momo close, uncaring that the charred head smeared ash over her uniform blouse. Now she knew why she was here at this school where everything was so different.

"Chiyo!" Hana shouted, running across the yard. "You didn't come to lunch. I was looking for you. Kimiko said you went to see the gardener's fire. What . . ." Her voice trailed off as she saw the charred doll in Chiyo's hand. "Oh, no! Oh, Chiyo! I'm so sorry!" Understanding darkened her eyes. "Hoshi."

Chiyo blinked hard. "I can't accuse her. Who would believe me? All I know is that I saw her walking this way and wondered why."

Hana looked at the gardener. "Maybe . . . ?"

"He didn't see her." Hana's stricken expression made Chiyo touch her hand, wanting to offer comfort. "Momo was sacrificed for a reason. Now I understand why I am here at Tsuchiura Girls' School."

"Why?" Hana looked as if she might not wish to hear the answer.

Chiyo smiled, but her mouth felt wrong, as if the smile might be a grimace. "I'm here to protect the American doll that will be coming to this school." She felt the rightness of it throughout her entire body. "I will never let Hoshi hurt a doll again."

CHAPTER 10

Chiyo couldn't accuse the general's daughter of burning her doll, so she brought the charred *kokeshi* to class in the morning and set it on a corner of her desk. By then, many of the girls had heard the story.

Hoshi's step faltered when she came into the classroom. The sweet smile on the eyeless doll looked as if it were hiding a secret. Kaito-sensei looked from Hoshi to Chiyo with her eyebrows rising.

"My doll must have fallen into the trash, Sensei," Chiyo explained. "I rescued her from the gardener's burn pile."

It could have been that way. Janitors were careful to remove the trash from classrooms even between classes. Everything at the school was kept immaculate.

But understanding came into the teacher's eyes. Maybe she was remembering the cushion thrown on the floor. Maybe she had also heard of the faked step in dance class. Chiyo could see Sensei's reasoning on her face. Kaito-sensei said nothing, but she did not order the doll removed from the desk.

At first, the *kokeshi* faced front. When Hana passed Chiyo's desk, she turned it to face Hoshi, as if the doll watched her with its silent, eyeless face. Chiyo met Hana's eyes and they both hid smiles.

Word flew like startled quail until everyone knew what had happened. Hana was not the only one who paused when passing Chiyo's desk to turn the burned *kokeshi* more squarely toward Hoshi.

Throughout the morning, the eyeless doll faced the general's daughter, whether she was at the corner table sharpening her slate pencil, working on the blackboard, or at her desk in back. Hoshi said nothing, but satisfaction warmed Chiyo whenever she saw the girl look away.

At the end of class, Kaito-sensei said quietly, "We have seen enough of the burned doll, Miss Tamura."

"*Hai*, Sensei." Gently, Chiyo placed the doll in a pocket of her uniform skirt. "Now she can rest."

Chiyo expected an attempt at revenge from Hoshi during dance class, but word must have reached Oki-sensei as well. Chiyo was placed in a different group of girls, where no one tried deliberately to confuse her.

In music class, Watanabe-sensei led them through singing "The Blue-Eyed Doll." "The song was written six years ago," he explained, "by a composer who wrote many songs, poems, and rhymes for Japanese children. He based the song on a doll from America."

As Sensei talked, Chiyo pictured the doll he described, a celluloid doll arriving on a ship with tears in her blue eyes. The doll didn't know the language and feared being lost. The song begged warmhearted Japanese girls to be her friends and play with her.

Chiyo cradled the burned *kokeshi* in her pocket, imagining how the celluloid doll felt, how all the dolls recently arriving in Yokohama must feel.

She would be one of those warmhearted girls and welcome any American doll given to the school. General Miyamoto was mistaken. To welcome the dolls was not weakness. She would do her best to see that no harm came to the new doll.

As she sang with the others, inviting the dolls to be her friends, she imagined the ship steaming across the rough sea. She knew that five ships had made room among their cargo for the dolls, each in her own crate with her suitcase, passport, and visa. In January, there must have been rain and wind, even lightning and crashing thunder. The brave dolls had survived all of that.

Chiyo put her heart into the words she sang, particularly through the line that said Japan, the land of Flowers, was now the doll's home.

How could Hoshi sing those words yet wish harm to the dolls?

When Sensei had led them through the song several times, he clapped his hands for attention. "Because the dolls arrived on a sad day in our history, the welcome in Yokohama was quieter than planned. Soon the dolls will enjoy a grand welcome in Tokyo."

Chiyo tried to imagine the ceremony, wishing she could see it.

Another girl with the same thought said aloud, "I wish we could be there."

"Ah." Sensei was not upset with the girl for speaking out of turn. His eyes glowed as he leaned forward. "Six of you will!"

The girls looked at one another. Whispering broke out. How could this be?

"Vocal groups will sing 'The Welcome Song' to the American dolls during the celebration in Tokyo." Sensei paused, letting anticipation build as the entire class appeared to hold its breath. "It is my great pleasure to announce that Tsuchiura Girls' School will send six girls to join the others."

The held breath let out at once. Now all the girls were whispering. No one could sit still. Some even spoke aloud. Who would be selected? Everyone believed that Hoshi would go, but all their faces glowed with the hope of being among the other five.

I have to be there. The thought pierced Chiyo. Someone needed to watch General Miyamoto's daughter. Deep inside, she feared that no one would.

But maybe I'll be chosen, too. Why not? Watanabe-sensei likes my singing. Fearing disappointment, she tried to push hope back. But she waited as eagerly as the others.

"Watanabe-sensei," Hoshi said. "Tamura Chiyo is new to our class. She does not know 'The Welcome Song' well. She would embarrass our school and should stay here."

This was Hoshi's answer to the watching *kokeshi*. Chiyo felt her heart sink. The rhythm of the welcome song carried her voice like the wind, but she *was* having trouble memorizing all the words. *Who will protect the dolls?*

Hana raised her hand. "Sensei, Miss Miyamoto is mistaken. Chiyo will know all the words. I am teaching them to her."

Sensei waved his hands for silence. "Miss Tamura's clear voice blends well with the rest of you. She will be considered when I make my selection. Now let us practice once again. I wish to hear joy in your voices."

Chiyo smiled at Hana as Hoshi's face became expressionless. The War of the Cushions had been joined by the War of the Welcome Song, though neither raged as fiercely as the War of the Burned *Kokeshi*.

In the days following Watanabe-sensei's announcement, Chiyo put her heart into the music lessons and practiced after school with Hana. She knew the others were practicing, too. In four days, Sensei would announce his decision. Impatience ran through the class.

The trip to Tokyo was all anyone talked about. In music class, every girl moved restlessly at her desk or sat forward on the edge of her chair. At last, the four days had passed. Watanabe-sensei prepared to write six names on the blackboard. As expected, Hoshi's was first. When Hana's name was added, Chiyo beamed at her friend. Another name went up and then another: Shizuko and Tomi, both girls who boarded at the school.

Chiyo could scarcely breathe. Only six girls were to go to Tokyo. Four were already listed. Everyone in class had become still. She could not look away from the board.

Sensei likes my voice. Her thoughts rang so loudly, she thought the others must hear. She didn't care. She had to be chosen. And why wouldn't she? She thought of the moment Headmaster had her sing for Watanabe-sensei and of Sensei's pleased reaction. *He said he wanted to work with me. He must add my name!*

Watanabe-sensei consulted a note in his hand, raised his chalk, and wrote again. Ito Kimiko.

Kimiko had been pleasant to her. Chiyo was pleased to see her listed.

Hoshi said in a near whisper, "Kimiko, plan to shop with me in Tokyo. I know where we can find kimono jackets pretty enough for the empress."

Chiyo only half-listened. One space was left. *It has to be me!* She clasped Momo so tightly between her hands, her fingers turned white. Time slowed, as if hours passed while she waited to see the final name placed on the board.

At last, Watanabe-sensei raised his chalk. He wrote: Fujii Michi.

CHAPTER 11

Chiyo sank back in her chair, her body going limp. She had tried to warn herself that she might not be selected. Now hope turned as black as her *kokeshi* doll's head.

"*Gomennasai*, Miss Tamura," Hoshi said in a pitying tone that was not sorry at all. "You must be so disappointed."

Chiyo wanted to force her face into a calm mask. *Thank you, Miss Miyamoto,* she would say. *You are kind.*

She could not do that. Her face would not shape itself into serenity. Sweet words would not rise to her lips. Instead, she put Momo back into her pocket and stared straight ahead. Why send the general's daughter to welcome the dolls when everyone had heard her say they should be destroyed?

To burn a small kokeshi *belonging to a farmer's daughter is a small offense,* Chiyo told herself. *To harm a doll sent in friendship and welcomed by the emperor is not. Even a general's daughter would never risk that.*

Yet uneasiness continued to run chill fingers along Chiyo's spine.

Michi raised her hand. "Sensei, what days will the group be away?"

Watanabe-sensei looked as excited as the class. "We will leave on Wednesday, the second of March, and stay with private families in Tokyo. The dolls' grand welcome will take place on March third."

"That's Hinamatsuri," Hoshi said.

"*Hai,* Miss Miyamoto," Sensei agreed. "The welcome will be held on the day traditionally celebrated by families with their heirloom *hina ningyo.* On Friday, we return here."

Michi spoke again, sounding close to tears. "I am so sorry. I cannot go. My grandmother is ill. She fears this will be her last Hinamatsuri. She wishes all her daughters and granddaughters to be with her. She has always loved that celebration."

As others murmured in sympathy, Michi rubbed her palms across her eyes. "*Sumimasen*, Sensei. I cannot go with you to Tokyo."

"Our sympathy is with you and your family, Miss Fujii," Sensei said gently.

Chiyo couldn't breathe. She felt sorry for Michi, but also as if she hovered above the classroom watching while Sensei erased the girl's name from the board. Chalk dust and suspense floated in the air. Someone must replace Michi.

Sensei looked at Hana. Was he about to choose her? Chiyo's hope sagged before she remembered that Hana was already on the list. "Miss Nakata," Sensei asked Hana, "are you a good teacher?"

"Yes!" Hana's quick smile brightened her entire face as she looked at Chiyo.

Had all the air been sucked from the room? There wasn't any left for breathing. Chiyo clutched Momo, not caring if charcoal smeared her pocket.

Sensei turned again to the blackboard. In quick, bold strokes, he filled the space left by the erasure: Tamura Chiyo.

She was sorry for Michi's disappointment, but in her mind, Chiyo leaped to her feet, shouting. *I'm going! I'm to help welcome the American dolls!*

She and Hana could talk of nothing else all that afternoon and evening and only settled to sleep when Mrs. Ogata insisted on silence.

The following morning, Watanabe-sensei called the six girls together after class to discuss the trip. They would travel by train. Oki-sensei would join them. But they would not be staying in private homes, after all. "General Miyamoto has arranged for all of you to share one large room in an esteemed hotel in Tokyo. Oki-sensei will stay with you, while I will spend the night nearby and join you in the morning."

Chiyo looked at Hana, hardly daring to believe this could be true. They were to ride in a train. And stay in a hotel. Until she came to Tsuchiura, Chiyo had never left her mountain village, never even dreamed of such adventure.

When Kaito-sensei dismissed them for lunch, Hana and Chiyo skipped across the courtyard. They didn't care who might see them behaving like five-year-olds. They were too excited to care.

"This is going to be the best time of our lives," Hana exclaimed.

Chiyo tried to picture a city the size of Tokyo. "Have you ever been there?"

"Yes, with my parents. There's so much to do.

Wait until you see all the things for sale. There's a lot to eat, too."

Chiyo thought of the coins Yamada-san had given her. "Do you think we will have time to look in the shops?"

"If we do, Oki-sensei will insist on going with us. She won't let any of us out of her sight in a city that big."

"I won't mind," Chiyo said, "as long as she doesn't make me practice dance in the street."

Hana laughed. "I can see you now." She spun around gracefully. "Bumping into everyone!"

Chiyo deliberately bumped into her and they both laughed. "Hoshi and Kimiko plan to shop," Chiyo said.

"They're used to the city, but I doubt Sensei will let them go alone."

"I hope not." Chiyo looked straight at Hana. "I want to keep an eye on Hoshi whenever she is near the American dolls."

"We will both watch her," Hana said, grinning. "That will add to the adventure!"

Hana could make an adventure of anything, Chiyo thought, and giggled. "Let's watch her now. Let's take our lunches and sit across the koi pond from Hoshi and her friends."

"And smile!" Hana exclaimed. "With one hand over our eyes to suggest the now sightless doll!"

Shrieking with laughter, they ran to the dining hall, where they had to be quieter, but kept looking at each other and giggling.

They each picked up a *bento* box, then hurried to the front of the school and picked a grassy spot directly across the pond from Hoshi.

Hoshi frowned, but it was Kimiko who called, "What are you two doing out here?"

"No room in the dining hall," Hana said, and smiled sweetly while covering her eyes.

Trying not to laugh, Chiyo smiled just as sweetly, with her eyes covered, too.

"You're acting like babies," Hoshi said. When Chiyo looked again, all three of the other girls had turned their kimonoed backs and were facing away from the pond.

It made the dried herring and pickled plums in their *bento* boxes taste that much better.

When they returned to Kaito-sensei's class, Chiyo still giggled whenever she met Hana's eyes. She tried hard to keep her attention on the kanji characters she was copying, but what were characters compared to the excitement of going to Tokyo?

Class had nearly ended for the day when Headmaster Hanarai's assistant stepped into the room and spoke briefly with Sensei.

Chiyo tried to tell herself that it had nothing to do with her. There was no reason for small hairs on her arms to be standing upright. Then Sensei looked directly at her. "Miss Tamura, you may be dismissed early. Someone is waiting for you in Headmaster Hanarai's office."

Someone? Chiyo's thoughts raced, providing answers each worse than the last. None prepared her to step into the office and see Yamada Nori.

CHAPTER 12

Chiyo stopped still while the assistant closed the door behind her. Every poorly done test and missed dance step, along with the burned-doll face aimed at Hoshi, slammed together in her head.

Yamada-san had been sitting in a chair before Headmaster's desk, talking with Hanarai-sensei. He stood the moment he saw her. Today, he wore a Western-style business suit of a dark blue jacket and trousers. A shiver ran through Chiyo. Was teasing Miss Miyamoto such a crime that the school had sent for Yamada Nori to take her away?

Chiyo desperately wanted to go home, but not in disgrace. *Hoshi deserved the teasing.* She did not think the men would listen to excuses.

No more than seconds had passed while frightening thoughts flashed through her head. She risked a swift glance at Yamada-san's face before she folded her hands and bowed. He looked pleasant, not angry. Maybe he was not here to remove her.

"You are surprised to see me, little sister," he said. "I must apologize for not sending word ahead. I've had business in Tokyo and decided to stop on my way home to learn how you are fitting in."

News of her teasing Hoshi had not yet reached him. Chiyo risked a glance at Headmaster Hanarai and was surprised to see him on his feet. "Take your time," he told Yamada-san. "I am needed in a meeting elsewhere."

Thankful for momentary escape, Chiyo returned her attention to the man who could take her home to her sister's wedding . . . or leave her here forever.

In a calm voice, Yamada-san asked, "Have you become friends with General Miyamoto's daughter?"

Maybe he did know of the teasing. Cautiously, she said, "We have several classes together. Miyamoto Hoshi is well mannered and liked by her teachers." Before he could ask again about friendship, she said, "My best friend is the daughter of a politician."

"Nakata Hana," he said. She wondered what else Headmaster had told him. "Miss Nakata is known to be a high-spirited girl indulged by her father and more likely to laugh at a problem than solve it."

"She has been kind to me since my first day here." She had had to leave Yumi behind. She would not stop playing with Hana.

"It is best to choose friends wisely. I hope you will keep this advice in mind." Without waiting for an answer, he turned to the headmaster's desk for a large box wrapped in red paper. "My younger daughter has outgrown this. I thought you might wear it for your sister's wedding, but I believe you may need it for school ceremonies."

Chiyo wiped her fingers on her skirt before daring to open the beautiful box. When she parted the tissue inside, rose silk glowed beneath. She lifted folds of rippling fabric, marveling over vibrant flowers hand-painted onto the cloth. "How beautiful!" Words were not enough. She could only look at him and hope that the glow in her face told him more than words could say.

Until this minute, she had expected to wear the borrowed school uniform to Tokyo. She folded the beautiful kimono back into its box. She had never owned anything so elegant.

"Your vocal teacher is greatly satisfied with your progress," Yamada-san said. "It pleases me to hear that."

Chiyo felt his words land on the good side of her mental scale. Excitement rushed through her. "I am to be one of six from the vocal group who will go to Tokyo to welcome the Friendship Dolls!"

"I am sorry, but you will not be going with them."

"What?" The word came out as a squeak.

"It is too soon for you to make such a trip." He looked regretful but firm. "The other girls are more sophisticated. You would be made unhappy. It is better you stay here and pay attention to your lessons."

She spoke as wistfully as she could manage, and the words sounded true because they were true. "I am sorry. The granddaughter of a shogun is to accept the first doll. I might have learned from her beautiful manners."

Yamada-san looked thoughtful. "I might permit you to go, if Miss Miyamoto requests your company."

That would never happen. Hopes that had barely risen scattered like leaves on the wind. Hoshi had insulted her when they met, humiliated her over the chair cushion, and deliberately confused her in dance. She had burned Momo!

Trying to keep despair from her voice, Chiyo said, "The general's daughter will never request the company of the daughter of a farmer. To do so would be to lose her father's respect."

Her chest felt squeezed and she drew a swift breath. "I do not have to be in Hoshi's small circle of friends to learn by observing the shogun's granddaughter."

He nodded. "An excellent argument." A flicker in his eyes reminded her that he, too, was a farmer. Again, she dared to hope and even to hide a smile.

What will Miyamoto Hoshi say if she learns that she is the reason I am to join the trip to Tokyo?

CHAPTER 13

As Chiyo stroked the box holding the kimono, Yamada-san asked, "Will there be time to shop in Tokyo?"

Chiyo's hands stilled. "Hoshi and Kimiko plan to shop."

In the same considering tone, Yamada-san said, "You will wish to buy a keepsake. Have you spent all the coins I gave you earlier?"

"No, Yamada-san." Relief rose through her. She had spent only a single sen, the one donated for the large dolls meant for the children in America. "I have most of them in my purse."

"Excellent. I could wish such frugality of my own two daughters. But do not be afraid to spend the coins, little sister. They are meant to be enjoyed."

In her home, money was not for pleasure, but for food and to help the family survive from one year to the next. Feeling as if she took rice from her mother's plate, she said, "I would like to surprise my mother with a small gift."

He nodded approval before warning, "Tokyo shops can be expensive. Do you have your purse with you?"

This time, she could give him the answer he wanted. "*Hai*, Yamada-san, I never leave it behind."

"You are wise. Open it, please."

She thought he meant to check her honesty, to see if the coins were really unspent. Why would he do that? She was always truthful.

When she opened the small purse, he poured a handful of coins onto those already there. *A treasure*, she thought, looking from the purse to Yamada-san in shock. She found her voice quickly. "*Arigatogozaimasu.*"

"Spend it with pleasure." He rose to his feet. She sprang to her own, rejoicing inside. She was going to Tokyo. She had coins to spend and a beautiful new kimono. Yamada Nori might be a good husband for her sister after all.

When Chiyo lifted the kimono from its wrappings later, sitting on her futon in the sleeping area, Hana clapped her hands. "It's perfect for your sister's wedding!"

"And for Tokyo!" Chiyo exclaimed. "Yamada-san almost said I couldn't go, but I told him I will learn from seeing the beautiful manners of a shogun's granddaughter."

She slid the silk through her fingers. Had anything in the whole entire world ever felt so soft? "I thought Yamada Nori was too old for Masako. Now I think she's lucky." She grinned at the other boarding girls in the room. "I think I'm lucky, too."

She realized that the girls were exchanging worried glances. They had all become silent. "Your kimonos are just as pretty," she said, sorry that she had seemed to boast and glad she hadn't told them about the money in the red silk purse.

"It's not that," Hana said. "None of us can wear kimonos. Sensei told us after you'd gone. Miss Tokugawa, the granddaughter of the shogun, is going to wear her school uniform. So we will, too, even Hoshi."

Chiyo tried to hide her disappointment as she folded the beautiful kimono into its wrappings. Hana touched her arm gently. "Think how nice it will be to have the kimono saved especially for your sister's wedding."

Hana's encouragement helped Chiyo smile. Yamada-san was wrong about Nakata Hana. She was a good friend.

As if to take her mind from disappointment, Shizuko said, "Did you know Mrs. Ogata once trained to be a geisha?"

Hana glanced cautiously toward the door. "I heard that she chose our rules from the ones she learned."

The girls all giggled. "'No talking with men outside of school or family,'" Shizuko said, adding, "Where would we find men to talk to?"

"'Speak softly and respectfully,'" Hana said, repeating another of the rules. "I admit to having trouble with that one at times."

Chiyo remembered another. "'Never show anger, jealousy, or visible emotion.' Hoshi learned that one well, but she inspires plenty of emotion in me!"

Hana laughed and tugged her blanket to her chin. Chiyo snuggled onto her own futon. She was beginning to fit in here. Maybe she would not disappoint her parents or Yamada Nori after all.

On the day they were to leave for Tokyo, excitement sparked through the classrooms. "A rickshaw is waiting outside!" Everyone crowded to peer through windows while teachers urged them to behave like young ladies.

"See! The driver waits beyond the gate."

"There's another!"

"And a third!"

The girls who weren't going were almost as excited as those who were. At last, the six with their two teachers settled into the wheeled carts and the drivers set off at a steady pace for the Tsuchiura train station.

"I have seen rickshaws before, but never ridden in one," Chiyo confided to Hana and Shizuko on either side of her.

"Next, a train!" Hana exclaimed.

Chiyo couldn't imagine such a thing. Her heart beat faster and she couldn't stop smiling. The six girls were a group now, she thought, sharing this special experience. She and Hoshi might even put their private wars behind them.

When they climbed from the rickshaws at the

station, Chiyo felt as if she had left her familiar world behind. While most of the group waited inside, she stood on the platform with Hana, peering eagerly down the tracks.

It seemed to take forever, but at last the great round nose of the train appeared far down the track, growing rapidly larger as it roared toward the station. Black smoke poured from the stack. The whistle blasted. *Come with me,* it urged in a breath-catching promise of adventure.

Chiyo bounced from one foot to the other. "There it is! Oh, Hana, there it is!"

The train chugged into the station, becoming a giant machine, huge and black and shuddering with power. They couldn't talk above the loud chuffing of the engine. The whistle, which sounded so filled with promise from a distance, made them cover their ears when it blasted nearby. Huge black wheels squealed to a stop. Metal bars banged and crashed.

The early-March wind caught steam from the stacks and flung it across the platform to billow around them. The engineer leaned from the window of his cab, waving as the engine moved past, bringing the passenger cars in line with the platform. The smell of hot metal washed from the wheels.

The teachers hurried from the station with the rest of the group and led them all down the line of windowed cars to the last. Metal steps rose from each side of a small platform with a waist-high railing across the end. From there, a door opened into the back of the car.

Hoshi and Kimiko were first to board, looking as if they rode a train every day. Tomi and Shizuko were next, their expressions solemn. Chiyo hung back, trying to take everything in, to remember it all for Yumi and her little sister, Kimi, before following Hana up the metal steps onto the train platform.

She paused, feeling the metal vibrate beneath her feet. When she looked down, she saw the tracks through cracks between the plates. The entire train was restless, like Yamada Nori's horse eager to be on its way. She turned to go inside the car.

Hoshi blocked the way. "Be careful, hill country girl. These platforms can be dangerous. I have heard of people falling onto the rails."

As Chiyo sucked in her breath, Hoshi looked hard into her eyes. "You would not be safe if caught back here while the wheels are turning." She stepped into the car. "It is so sad, Miss Tamura, that you do not fit in with the rest of us."

"Hana doesn't agree with you," Chiyo exclaimed.

Hoshi's perfect eyebrows lifted slightly. "Dear Hana. Like her father, she loves to take up lost causes." She turned away, adding, "Sometimes it's best to leave the lost cause where it belongs."

The warning against falling under the wheels was meant to scare me, Chiyo told herself as Hoshi's graceful steps carried her deeper into the car. But she followed quickly, glad to leave the platform.

Hana called, "I saved you a seat by the window."

As Chiyo slid gratefully into the far seat, Hana leaned close to ask, "What did Hoshi want?"

Chiyo smiled with her teeth together. "Hoshi is worried about my safety. She warned me that the train platform can be dangerous."

"She is thoughtful," Hana said, her tone as sarcastic as Chiyo's. But her eyes grew serious. "Be careful, Chiyo. Do not be alone out there."

The train whistle blasted again. Heavy connectors banged together. The wheels began to turn. Hana leaned across Chiyo to peer through the window while the entire train throbbed with energy.

To Chiyo, it was a great pulsing creature of

steel and steam meant to carry them all the way to Tokyo, wheels clattering and cars swaying. Beyond the window, fields and houses swept by. Yamada Nori's horse and carriage had not traveled so fast.

Chiyo laughed aloud with joy. *Okaasan* had been right. Life was changing. Who in her village had ever traveled by train? Probably no one.

As time passed, Hana sank back in her seat, but Chiyo leaned into the window, eager for her first sight of Tokyo.

Another small village came into view. The train chugged to a stop for three people waiting on the platform. The door at the back of Chiyo's car swung open to admit a woman carrying a basket of oranges. She held one out. "Only one sen!"

Hana was sleeping. It would be fun to surprise her with an orange to share. Hadn't Yamada-san said the coins were for pleasure? Chiyo brought her purse from a skirt pocket and picked through for a sen.

The woman moved quickly through the car. People slept or talked, paying no attention. As the vendor returned to the back platform, Chiyo called, "Wait, please. I would like to buy an orange."

The train whistle swallowed her voice, and the door closed after the woman. Chiyo stepped over a small basket blocking the aisle and hurried to the train platform.

She was too late. The woman was off the train. The whistle blasted again and the huge iron wheels began to turn, picking up speed, faster and faster.

Chiyo clung to the back rail. Trees and homes pulled away at dizzying speed. Out here, the rumble and clatter and whistle blasts were even louder. Smoke and ashes swept around the sides of the train and into her face and hair, making her cough while her skirt and blouse whipped against her body.

The short distance from the platform rail to the safety of the car looked huge with the ground flying by at either side. She gathered her courage, then lunged from her grip on the rail to wrench the door handle. It didn't move. The door was locked.

CHAPTER 14

Chiyo pressed her face to the window. All the seats faced toward the engine. No one looked back toward her.

She pounded one hand on the glass and shouted, "Hello!" Her voice could not be heard over the blast of the whistle and the clatter of wheels on the rails.

Hana must still be sleeping. She at least would have missed her.

Hoshi and Kimiko talked together, looking as if neither had moved since leaving Tsuchiura. Someone had locked the door. It couldn't have locked itself. Unless the latch had slipped. Could that happen?

Chiyo slid down to sit on the platform against the door, more sheltered from the wind. She rubbed an ashy spot on her skirt, wondering if it would ever be clean again. She had to wear it for the Welcome Ceremony.

Why was she thinking of the ceremony? She was trapped out here while her head reeled with Hoshi's warning that people sometimes fell.

Chiyo huddled closer to the door. *I thought the six of us were becoming a family, sharing this wonderful experience. But we're not a family. We're not even a good group.*

And the experience wasn't so wonderful anymore.

The wheels rolled even faster. The train rattled and swayed. To one side, cows grazed and were gone. The train crossed a bridge she saw only when it was behind them. She spit out ash. She could not stay here all the way to Tokyo.

Carefully, she got to her feet and looked through the window again. She was surprised to see her teachers and some of the students standing. There was Hana, looking frightened and peering under seats. Shizuko and Tomi had opened windows and were leaning out, looking back.

They couldn't see the platform. She thought of

leaning around the end of the train, but the railing didn't cover the stairs. There was nothing safe to hold on to. She moved back to the window. Why didn't anyone look this way?

If they couldn't find her, would they stop the train? Would the engineer back it up, looking for her? The platform might jerk and toss her onto the rails!

She peered harder through the heavy glass, her nose almost touching it. How could she catch someone's eye? Her uniform was dark. So was her hair.

She thought of the red silk purse Yamada Nori had given her and fished it from a pocket while clinging to the door handle. It was going to be filthy. That couldn't be helped.

She waved the red purse frantically against the glass. The clasp came open. Coins spilled out, bouncing and rolling around her feet. She darted after them, grabbing too late as her largest coin bounced down the steps and away. Three smaller coins followed.

"No! Noooo!"

Those are gone, her thoughts warned. *Save the rest!*

She sank to her knees, throwing her skirt wide

to cover spinning coins. Tears threatened, and she wiped them away. Hoshi was not going to see tear tracks on her face.

She was afraid to lift her skirt to see if any coins were saved. How could she tell Yamada Nori that his money jumped off the train?

She wanted to blame someone. She wanted to blame Hoshi, who must have locked her out here. *But I was the one who chased the orange vendor.*

Money should be saved, not spent on pleasure. Yamada Nori was wrong. In my village, even a sen is precious. And now I've lost all that he gave me.

The mental scale weighed heavily on the bad-conduct side. But she would not sit here feeling sorry for herself. She reached for her skirt to look for trapped coins.

The door swung inward. Oki-sensei grabbed her arm and hauled her to her feet. The remaining coins spun, with sen and rin flying off the platform.

"My money!"

"Your safety is my concern. What are you doing out here?"

Chiyo lunged for a golden yen—a yen!—near her shoe, but the teacher yanked her inside the car. "Answer me! You had us all frantic! Why were you out there?"

Chiyo looked back in anguish. "I wanted an orange. My money fell on the platform! Sensei, it's all I have!"

"Take your seat, Miss Tamura. Now."

Chiyo stumbled to her row. "Someone locked the door," she told Hana, gulping back tears she would not shed. "Most of my money bounced off the train and the rest is on the platform!"

"Miss Tamura," Sensei warned again. "Sit down."

Hana exclaimed, "Someone locked her out there!"

Sensei's mouth got thin. "Did you see someone lock the door, Miss Nakata?"

"No, but Chiyo was locked out."

"We will blame the wind or a faulty latch." Oki-sensei's tone forbade argument. "Miss Tamura is now safely inside, where she will remain. The matter is closed."

"Not to me!" Hana said with fire still in her voice.

Oki-sensei returned to her seat beside Watanabe-sensei and frowned all the girls into facing forward.

Hana said fiercely to Chiyo, "It was Hoshi!"

"We think that because of her threat." Feeling hollow inside, Chiyo stared out the window. She remembered Yamada-san warning that Miss Nagata was known to be high-spirited. After losing her money, she didn't want to get Hana in trouble, too.

"We'll get even with her," Hana said, as if hearing the thought. "You wait! We will!"

Chiyo drew a deep breath, longing to run to the door to see if even one sen remained. In her mind, she pictured all her coins bumping and spinning off the platform, but one might be lying flat. The yen might still be there. She would look carefully when they left the train in Tokyo.

I am not here to shop, she reminded herself. *I'm here for the American dolls. I don't need shopping to make sure Hoshi doesn't hurt one of them.*

CHAPTER 15

As they approached Tokyo, Chiyo marveled at thatched-roof homes stretching to either side. "They're as close together as a farmer's cabbages."

Hana laughed. "I'm glad you're able to smile again."

"This might be my only chance to see the city," Chiyo answered. "I'm not going to ruin it over coins I didn't expect to have in the first place." But she couldn't help wishing that she could have given a nice gift to her parents.

The thatched homes gave way to taller buildings. Soon the train pulled into Tokyo Station, billowing steam. Wheels shrieked as the cars lurched, forcing those in the aisles to clutch seat backs. Chiyo stumbled toward the aisle. She meant to be first to the platform at the back, but a large woman with a basket stepped in front of her, then let everyone ahead into the aisle, including Hoshi and Kimiko.

Chiyo's stomach clenched. She wasn't even surprised to hear Hoshi exclaim loudly, "Look, Kimiko! A shiny new yen. Maybe it will bring me luck!"

Hana shouted past Chiyo's shoulder, "You know that belongs to Chiyo!" But the train whistle blew, a fresh burst of steam blasted in from the open door, and everyone still aboard hurried to reach the station platform.

Chiyo resisted a need to shove past them all. Rude behavior might be reported to Headmaster, and that side of the scale was getting heavier.

Hana said, "We should tell Sensei."

Chiyo shook her head. There wasn't anything she could do except add another mark against Hoshi's name in her mind.

When they stood on the station platform, the smell of smoke and hot metal made their noses wrinkle. Oki-sensei bustled about, locating luggage and guiding the girls into waiting rickshaws. As their bearer hurried them through crowded city streets, Chiyo, Hana, and Tomi sat together, pointing out one sight after another. Automobiles rumbled past, startling Chiyo with their speed and power. And what was coming along the street now?

"It's an electric streetcar," Oki-sensei called from the rickshaw ahead as a large vehicle whizzed past on tracks laid in the street. It looked scary to Chiyo. People sat on long benches facing the street while the car traveled rapidly along. How did they keep from falling off?

Shop windows held more goods than she had ever imagined. *Hina ningyo* for a Hinamatsuri display posed on the tiers of a crimson-draped stand in one window; there were even more dolls and accessories than she had seen in Yamada Nori's home that night.

A bicyclist pedaling past blocked the view with many bamboo birdcages roped together behind and above him. Smells crowded the air until it was impossible to tell one from another. Chiyo thought she smelled fresh yuzu and soy sauce among a mixture of aromas from herbs and roasting meats. Vendors busy with small hibachis offered skewers of cooked meats and vegetables to people passing by.

Chiyo recognized the smell of river water and wet green plants when the rickshaws traveled across a wide bridge. Below, large and small boats, many with sails, crowded the water and lined both shores. Hana said, "Some of those boatmen have traveled from Tsuchiura to sell their goods. The journey takes a strong wind and days of travel."

Yumi and Kimi would never believe all she was seeing, and the trip had barely begun.

When the rickshaws stopped, Oki-sensei pronounced their hotel to be satisfactory, although she had once stayed at the Grand Hotel in Yokohama. As they gathered in the lobby, she told them sadly that the great Kanto earthquake four years before had destroyed the Grand, along with much of the harbor and city. In her mind, no other hotel could compare with that lost grandeur.

This was grand enough for Chiyo. She glanced at Hoshi and tried to walk through the lobby with the same straight spine and graceful steps. It was hard to keep her eyes down while longing to look from side to side.

Golden tatami mats floored a room vast enough to hold her entire house and maybe Yumi's as well. How could Oki-sensei keep saying that this hotel could never compare with the majestic Grand?

"Do you know a famous American writer named Rudyard Kipling stayed there?" Sensei asked. "As well as several well-known actors? The guests today . . ." She glanced at a group wearing western clothes and shook her head. "They cannot compare."

Chiyo couldn't help casting quick glances after the group in western clothing. *Otousan* wore soft trousers and a loose tunic to work in the fields, but those were nothing like the suits of fine cloth and closer fit on the men here.

Yamada Nori had worn such clothing at the school. He must have been as comfortable in Tokyo as in Tsuchiura. Was Masako adventurous enough to live in two worlds? *I will have so much to tell my sister when I see her again.*

When the group reached an upstairs hallway, Hana grabbed Chiyo's hand. "Run!"

Startled, Chiyo raced with her to an open doorway where young men were taking the luggage. Hana pulled her past them to a corner window and onto a futon. "Hoshi will expect to sleep near the windows."

"Too late," Chiyo said, flinging herself flat.

The rest of the group soon came into the room. While Oki-sensei dealt with the luggage, Hoshi walked over to Chiyo and Hana. "This corner is mine."

Chiyo sat beside Hana and smiled sweetly, both of them closing their eyes in their burned-doll look.

"Ohh!" Hoshi stalked over to the others. "Sensei, my father paid for the room. He expects me to have the view."

Sensei waved away the luggage carriers, looking distracted. "Fortunately, you are too polite to complain, Miss Miyamoto. And after all, you were not the first to claim the spot."

Hoshi's shocked expression made Chiyo turn away to hide laughter. Hana leaned close. "Sensei knows who locked you on the train platform, but she won't risk General Miyamoto's outrage to say so. He would never believe that his perfect daughter would do such a thing."

Chiyo hadn't realized that Hoshi's spiteful act could cause a problem for their teacher. For the first time, she understood why Sensei had said that since Chiyo was safely inside the train, the matter was closed.

But she was uneasy about claiming the space with the view. "Won't Sensei expect to sleep near the windows?"

"She'll sleep nearest the door to be sure we all stay inside. You'll see."

Chiyo lay back on the soft futon, thinking how much nicer it was than her sleeping mat at home. She meant to enjoy every minute of this trip, but she would sleep with one eye open, in case Hoshi decided to accidentally drop a cushion over her face and sit on it.

CHAPTER 16

Sliding paper *fusuma* screens divided the large room into sections. As Hana had expected, Oki-sensei chose an area near the doorway.

Watanabe-sensei met the group for a short walk to a noodle house for lunch. When Hoshi raised her bowl to her lips, pushed noodles forward with her chopsticks, and slurped them in, Chiyo suspected her of a trick. But everyone at the table was slurping their noodles and broth. She had supposed that only country people ate in such a rapid manner.

Free to enjoy her lunch, she raised her bowl to her mouth. Hana nudged her, looking toward three women wearing short skirts at a nearby table. Their hair, cut in short black wings, swung against their ears whenever they turned their heads.

All three brought out cigarettes. Smoke soon rose from their red lips and formed a smelly cloud.

"Flappers." Oki-sensei put one hand to her heavy chignon as if to reassure herself it was still there, then leaned forward to warn in a low voice, "Notice how those young women draw attention to themselves. They are neither graceful nor attractive. You girls do not want to be like them."

Chiyo concentrated on her noodles and broth to keep from staring at the women. Hana must have peeked, however. She murmured, "How strange their hair must feel swinging against their faces."

Masako now wore her hair in a divided chignon. When she married, she would arrange it into a single round bun to show that her heart was one with her husband's. Softly, Chiyo asked, "How can anyone know from such a style whether they are married or single?"

"No one would marry such women," Hoshi said. "They must all be without husbands."

Both teachers nodded agreement.

Above the sounds of people enjoying their noodles, parts of the women's conversation reached

Chiyo. Their words startled her even more than their loud voices.

The flappers all worked in a business office. How was that possible? Wasn't business for men? The women laughed often and didn't bother to lower their eyes when a man walked past.

Shizuko cast a sidewise glance. "How sad that they behave so freely."

Shizuko was beginning to sound like Hoshi, Chiyo thought. *I wish to be as graceful as Hoshi, but I will never think like her.*

Oki-sensei drew their attention. "We have an afternoon free. I will escort any of you who would like to shop."

As they made excited plans, Chiyo remained silent. Hana turned to her. "You can come, Chiyo. You can enjoy looking at everything."

That didn't sound like fun to Chiyo. She didn't want to remember her lost coins while everyone else bought sweets or souvenirs.

Oki-sensei said quietly, "Miss Tamura, you might like to use the time to write to your parents. You may take a sheet of paper and an envelope from those in my trunk."

Chiyo thought of her parents' pleasure and surprise on receiving a letter from her. Would a mail carrier make a special trip to the village? Maybe Yamada Nori would stop by the school again and she could send it with him.

"*Arigatogozaimasu,*" she told the teacher. "They will be pleased to hear from me."

Upstairs, the girls gathered jackets and purses and rushed away while Oki-sensei selected paper for Chiyo along with a fresh nub for her pen and a box of ink.

While Sensei hurried after the others, Hoshi paused beside Chiyo. "I am sad to see you forced to remain in the room alone. I can spare one sen for you to spend."

Hoshi would enjoy watching me look at the prices of things I can't buy, Chiyo warned herself. *Even if I could buy something for a sen, Hoshi would remind me of her generosity through the entire trip.* "You are generous, but I will stay and write to my parents."

"As you wish." As Hoshi started for the door, a very young maid came in with towels piled in her arms. "Girl," Hoshi said in a manner suited to an empress. "Can't you see the room is occupied?"

The maid bowed her head. She looked even younger than Masako, maybe no more than fifteen or sixteen. Chiyo wondered if this was her first job.

"Hoshi, she must have thought we were all out shopping."

"For her own good, the girl needs to learn that guests must not be interrupted by housekeepers."

"*Gomennasai*," the girl apologized, keeping her head low.

"What is your name?" Hoshi asked. "The hotel management should know they have untrained employees."

The maid hunched her shoulders. She had become very pale. In a soft voice, she answered with her last name, as everyone did. "I am Toyama, miss."

Could Hoshi's complaint cost the girl her job? Chiyo knew how important work could be when a family depended on the income, and she could not keep silent. "She is just doing her work."

"It is our duty to train her to do it right." Hoshi permitted herself a superior expression. "Not that you would know. I'm afraid you are only fit to be her, not to be served by her."

Chiyo had let Hoshi's insults roll off since meeting her, but someone had to speak for the maid. "Toyama is not at fault. She brought the extra towels for me. I knew you would use too many."

Stepping forward, she took the towels from the girl's trembling hands. "*Arigatogozaimasu*, Toyama."

A man spoke from the open doorway into the hall. "My daughter, you have learned a lesson. A leader gathers all the facts before speaking."

"*Otousama!*" Hoshi exclaimed, using the formal expression for her father and bowing with deep respect. "I did not expect you, *Otousama*."

Chiyo bowed, too, feeling awkward with towels in her arms and glad to glimpse the maid slipping from the room. General Miyamoto looked as if a smile never challenged the severe line of his mouth. He wore a sharply pressed uniform with many medals over his chest, but it was his expression that made her shiver.

Her own father had looked at her with disapproval many times, yet she had always seen love in his eyes. There was no tenderness in General Miyamoto. Had he come to visit his daughter? Or was he here to see if she was behaving as he expected? Chiyo didn't want to feel sympathy for Hoshi. But she did. Her own father would never shame his daughter before another.

"There is a second lesson here," General

Miyamoto continued, as if offering a lecture to a group slow in learning. "A leader does not gain power by abusing those who serve."

Hoshi looked as if she were keeping herself humble with an effort, her body stiff and her head down. *She will never forgive me for seeing her humiliated,* Chiyo realized, and, like the maid, quietly eased from the room.

CHAPTER 17

When General Miyamoto joined the group for dinner, Hoshi glowed with pride. She sat near her father, looked at him often, and gazed kindly at the others as if she were empress and they her people.

The teachers appeared to agree with every word the general uttered. Chiyo's fingers tightened around her chopsticks when he said of the dolls, "Let us hope our emperor has a reason for this exchange. When we welcome toys from a country we may someday wish to include in our empire, our country appears weak. Japan must show strength our enemies will recognize."

Chiyo kept her gaze on her plate so no one would see rebellion sparking in her eyes. Why would Japan want to invade a country so far away?

She was glad to hear Watanabe-sensei object even in a mild manner. "We noticed posters welcoming tourists posted at the rail station."

The general chuckled. "I believe you have discovered the emperor's reasoning. First, welcome their tourist money, then . . ." He left the word *invasion* to everyone's imagination, but it was there in his voice.

He has been too long in the military, Chiyo thought. *I am beginning to understand Hoshi, and even to pity her a little.*

She was glad to unroll her futon and blanket soon afterward, with the *fusuma* screen between sleeping spaces closing her away from everyone but Hana.

She dreamed of dolls crowded onto the deck of a ship. They were smiling and waving toward the shore. Their blue eyes sparkled and blond curls bounced. But then General Miyamoto appeared on the dock. He pointed sternly to the water, and the ship with all the dolls sank beneath the waves.

What did that mean? Chiyo wondered on waking. Horrified, she shook her head to clear the dream away.

Watanabe-sensei joined them for breakfast as he had promised, followed by a rickshaw tour of Tokyo. This time, Chiyo noticed Western smells that were stronger than the lime, soy sauce, and drying herbs she expected. Tobacco smoke made her nose wrinkle, but the tempting aroma of chocolate was as strong. She breathed that in with pleasure, almost tasting the creamy dark sweetness.

The tour ended at a noodle house, where they sipped green tea and enjoyed bowls of plump noodles with many vegetable and fish toppings offered in small lacquered side dishes.

"You girls have been patient," Oki-sensei said as they sipped the last of their tea. "Are you ready to see the American dolls?"

"Yes!" Chiyo clapped one hand over her mouth. The word had burst out.

Hoshi's lips tilted with superior amusement.

"A few rules must be discussed," Oki-sensei warned. "Under no circumstances are any of you to touch the dolls. We will walk past the display and admire only with our eyes. I do not wish to see any one of you put even a finger on a doll."

Watanabe-sensei leaned forward. "The ceremony will take place in a building near the beautiful Meiji Shrine. Many children will be present, both from the American school in Tokyo and from our schools, with speeches and songs from both countries."

Chiyo had not heard that American children were in Tokyo. She listened in surprise as Sensei explained that the Americans had their own school. Would they have blond hair? She was sure the dolls would be blond, with eyes so blue, you could almost see into their heads.

"Where will the dolls go after today?" Kimiko asked.

"The little doll messengers will be displayed for a short time, then taken to primary schools and kindergartens throughout the country."

"We'll get one, won't we?" Hana asked.

"We may. Sadly, there are not enough for each school in Japan to receive a doll, but the schools chosen will each hold welcoming ceremonies."

If she had not been sent to Tsuchiura, she would have missed so much, Chiyo marveled. She could hardly remember why she had first resisted Yamada Nori's decision to send her to school.

As Watanabe-sensei sat back, Oki-sensei said, "You should all be very proud. Not only are you representing Tsuchiura Girls' School, today you are becoming part of history."

Hoshi spoke in a pleasant tone with an edge that echoed her father. "It is to be hoped that history will not call us foolish."

Watanabe-sensei frowned. "Please do not be negative, Miss Miyamoto. Today is for celebrating. We will *all* take part."

"*Hai*, Sensei." Hoshi bowed her head but added, "Let us hope there is no explosive in a doll set to blow up in the hands of the welcoming girls." Everyone looked at her in horror. She kept her eyes down, her expression serene, and said no more.

"There is no explosive," Chiyo whispered to Hana. "Hoshi wants to ruin the day for all of us."

Oki-sensei said firmly, "Girls, you will clear your minds of unpleasant thoughts."

CHAPTER 18

As bearers pulled their rickshaws down the street, Chiyo felt as if she had waited for this day her entire life. She was amazed by the number of automobiles. Near the hall, motors rumbled as if demons gathered, all of them thunderous with smoky exhaust.

Hundreds of girls gathered inside the hall. Huge Japanese and American flags decked the wall beyond a cloth-draped table arranged for speakers.

Chiyo looked curiously at the girls from the American school in Tokyo. "How tall they are," she murmured to Hana.

"Their bright clothes make them look even taller." Hana glanced down at her own dark dress and long dark stockings, the uniform worn by all the girls from Tsuchiura. Many of the American girls wore colorful dresses with white stockings to their knees and shiny black shoes with straps across their ankles.

Most had brown or blond hair, but the blue eyes Chiyo saw were not like windows into their owners' heads as she had wondered about the American dolls. She couldn't decide whether she felt relief or disappointment.

Before the ceremony began, they were all invited to walk past the tables where dolls slept in their crates. They were only a few of the thousands sent from America. The girls filed past, pausing to admire each doll, some with golden curls, others with brown.

Letters written in English accompanied each doll, with Japanese translations beside them. A photographer moved among the tables, pausing to set some of the dolls upright for better pictures.

Chiyo paused before a beautiful doll with golden curls and a friendly smile. When she took time to read the translated letter, the rest of her group pushed on past. She didn't care. She would never have a chance like this again.

The doll's passport said her name was Emily

Grace. "You are the prettiest one," Chiyo whispered to her. The letter was signed by a girl named Lexie and included a haiku.

My doll travels far.
Her arms open wide for hugs.
Will blossoms greet her?

"Yes, they will," Chiyo promised. "We are celebrating Hinamatsuri. You will see peach orchards filled with blossoms." A second haiku had been tucked beside the letter. Chiyo decided she liked it best.

Emily Grace glows.
Her warm smile carries friendship.
Sunlight after rain.

Someone shouted, "Look out!"

Bomb! Chiyo thought, as Hoshi's suggestion flashed through her head. In the same moment, the doll began to topple. Realizing that someone had bumped the display, Chiyo grabbed the falling doll while the box, suitcase, and passport flew to the floor.

As if waking from her long sea voyage, Emily Grace opened her dark-lashed blue eyes. They looked directly into Chiyo's. In a sweet, clear voice, the doll said, "Mama."

Okaasan. That was what the word *Mama* meant. For Chiyo, everything else disappeared, even the white flashes from bulbs in dozens of cameras. In that moment, her heart melted. Love for Emily Grace flooded in, crowding out everything.

"You are the sweetest doll in the world," Chiyo told her. "Oh, how I hope you will come to my school."

As she shifted the doll in her arms, Emily Grace said again, "Mama."

Chiyo held her close, gazing into the doll's blue eyes with all the longing she felt inside. "Your journey is over," she whispered. "You are home."

A camera flashed. She was barely aware of it until Hoshi's voice cut in. "Sensei, Chiyo is holding a doll! She has forgotten not to touch them!"

Oki-sensei exclaimed, "Miss Tamura! Replace that doll at once!"

Chiyo felt dazed, as if returning from somewhere far away. The teacher's shock and Hoshi's secret smile were sharp reminders. "She was falling, Sensei. Someone bumped her box."

The box was back on the table. Chiyo placed Emily Grace carefully inside.

Oki-sensei made her way past several girls to pull Chiyo from the display. "You will sit in a chair along the side of the room and watch the ceremony. You will not sing with the others."

Not sing? After all her practice? Chiyo wanted to sing a welcome especially for Emily Grace.

"She fell," she repeated, bowing. "Someone called a warning. I caught her." Oki-sensei would not yield. Chiyo realized that the teacher was embarrassed that one of her girls had been seen holding a doll.

Should I have let Emily Grace smash on the floor? She bit back the words. Arguing with the teacher would not help, but she seethed with the unfairness as Hana appeared beside her.

"Who called a warning?" Hana asked.

"A girl. I didn't know her voice."

"Was Hoshi nearby?"

"Hoshi!" Chiyo laughed, though she wasn't amused. "Hoshi never shouts. Besides, she hates the dolls. She wouldn't have called a warning. She'd have let Emily Grace fall and hope to see her break."

Hana shook her head. "Don't you see what

happened? Hoshi shouted the warning. She meant for you to catch the doll so she could blame you for touching it. She probably pushed the box herself, to get you in trouble. Let's go tell Sensei what really happened."

Chiyo shook her head. "I may be a girl from a hill farm, but even I have learned that Sensei will not confront General Miyamoto's daughter."

Trying to bury resentment, she walked past the rows of seated girls and sank onto a low bench at one side. But she wasn't sorry to have held Emily Grace, even for a little while.

CHAPTER 19

Chiyo sat carefully, with her feet together and her hands clasped in her lap. She meant to do nothing more to upset her teachers. If a report reached Yamada-san that she had broken the rule and touched a doll, she hoped he would also hear that she sat dutifully quiet afterward.

Hundreds of girls filled the audience: Chiyo saw students of all ages. Bulbs flashed as photographers shot picture after picture. Men from newspapers and even from magazines moved through the crowd with notebooks and pencils.

After opening speeches, everyone but Chiyo sang first the Japanese and then the American anthems.

The music soared through Chiyo, causing her pain as well as pleasure. Her voice could not be among the others, though she had done nothing wrong.

After more speeches, the audience stirred with fresh interest. An American girl wearing a white ruffled dress and bonnet walked onto the stage. She was Miss Betty Ballantine, the American ambassador's seven-year-old daughter, who spoke in Japanese, bringing greetings from the children of America. Chiyo thought her words were sweet and presented without shyness in front of all these people.

Forty-eight American girls lined up on one side of the stage, holding forty-eight dolls to represent each American state. Across from them, forty-eight girls from Japanese schools stood in respectful ranks. Chiyo felt her heart beat faster, as if she were one of them, though no one from her school was onstage.

As the American girls' voices rose in the "Doll Song," Chiyo looked with longing toward Emily Grace, still on the long table with the others.

Then Miss Tokugawa Yukiko, who was descended from the last of the shoguns, walked to the center of the stage. Chiyo leaned forward as if a few inches could help her see better.

Chiyo liked Miss Tokugawa's dark pleated skirt

and matching jacket better than Miss Ballantine's bright white ruffles. Yukiko's black hair shining in the light looked far nicer than the ruffles covering Betty's head. To Chiyo, the bright white seemed to shout, *Look at me! Here I am!* Yukiko knew that people would see her. She didn't need to wear white.

Are girls from our two countries so different? Chiyo wondered. Yet they all loved dolls and welcomed friendship. *Well, most of them,* she corrected herself, remembering Miyamoto Hoshi.

Betty Ballantine presented the doll representing all of America to Miss Tokugawa. How gracefully seven-year-old Yukiko received the doll. *I could learn better manners in five minutes with her,* Chiyo thought, *than in an hour spent watching Hoshi.*

Pride glowed through her as each Japanese girl accepted a doll and cradled it carefully. Miss Tokugawa presented greetings from Japanese children. Then it was time to sing "The Welcome Song" to the dolls.

Chiyo ached with unfairness. *I sit here like part of the wall. Because of Miyamoto Hoshi.*

I will not let Hoshi stop me!

Sensei wouldn't interrupt the program, and Chiyo didn't care what happened after that. She sprang to her feet and let her voice ring out with the others, putting into the song all that she was feeling, especially when she reached the last words, "*We will all love you and be nice to you.*"

As the song faded, a young man leaned against the wall nearby. A large camera hung from a strap over one of his shoulders. "You have a pretty voice," he said softly while the American ambassador prepared to speak. "You sing the words as if they come from your heart."

"*Arigatogozaimasu,*" she whispered. Mrs. Ogata's rules flashed through her head. *No talking to men.*

"I'd wager the dolls liked the song," the man said. "They've come a long way."

"*Hai.*" She answered without meaning to, but she hoped the dolls had heard her singing.

"What did you whisper to that one doll?" he asked. "The one you were holding?"

Chiyo gazed at her hands, but he smiled when everyone else had frowned at her and he didn't sound as if he blamed her.

In her silence, he said, "You were quick to catch her when she fell. Your teacher should be proud of you."

She looked at him then, to see if he had a Hoshi expression, but he looked as if he meant his words.

He might have been the only friendly person in this entire hall, and she didn't want to be rude. What was the rest of that rule? *No talking to men outside of school and family.*

This was school, in a way. She spoke to the fingers she twisted in her lap. "I told her, 'You are home.'"

"You are home," he repeated. "You have a kind heart. I am glad to know you, Miss . . . ?"

"Tamura Chiyo." Her name was out before she thought twice. Now it was too late to call it back. But what harm could come of telling him her name? She hoped he wouldn't ask why she was sitting here alone.

The American ambassador began his speech, saying, "This day will be remembered as one that helped forge friendship between the two countries, friendship that will never be broken."

Chiyo hoped that Hoshi would take those words to her father, but he would probably have something unpleasant to say about them. What if others felt like General Miyamoto? Chiyo longed to hold Emily Grace one last time.

A band played while women from the American Association carried baskets of candy through the audience. Chiyo followed them with her eyes, wondering if any of the women would notice her sitting at the side.

"We can't let you be overlooked," the photographer said, startling her. She had almost forgotten he was there. "Wait here, Tamura Chiyo." He walked swiftly to the nearest American woman.

When he returned with a packet for her, Chiyo thanked him shyly. Candy wouldn't make up for the sorrow she felt in leaving without Emily Grace, but it was nice, and something she rarely tasted. She held the packet in her lap until the photographer moved away.

As she unwrapped a hard lemon ball, Oki-sensei hurried to her.

"You may rejoin the girls from Tsuchiura." Oki-sensei looked over at the photographer with an even sterner frown than she had given Chiyo for catching the doll. With one hand on Chiyo's arm, she hurried her toward her group.

On the way back to the hotel, Chiyo kept thinking of Emily Grace. She hadn't expected to love the doll, but she missed her as if she had known her always. She sat twisting the candy packet in her hands while, to either side, her friends exclaimed over the flavors.

At dinner and all through the rest of the evening, the girls talked about the ceremony. "Did you see Miss Ballantine when she offered the doll representing America to Miss Tokugawa? What a pretty ruffled dress she wore."

"Did you think it pretty?" That was Hoshi. "I thought it looked showy. A girl should not draw attention to herself."

Kimiko said mildly, "As a representative of her country, she was there to be noticed."

Chiyo did not join the conversation. She was glad to climb onto her futon and welcome sleep. Maybe by tomorrow, her disgrace for touching the doll would be forgotten.

She woke hours later, with early-morning sunlight streaming into the room and Hana leaping onto the futon beside her. "Chiyo! Chiyo! Wake up! Your picture! It's in the newspaper! You're famous!"

CHAPTER 20

"What?" Chiyo tried to sit up. "You're squashing me. Move!"

"Come and see!" Hana scrambled to her feet. "Oki-sensei is not pleased, but she never is. Hurry, Chiyo!"

"Wait! What's going on?"

Again urging, "Hurry," Hana slipped past the *fusuma* screen.

Newspaper? Hana's words flared into Chiyo's mind. She was in a newspaper? How could that be true—it couldn't be—but if it was, what would Yamada Nori think?

Whatever he thought, it wouldn't be good. If she was really in the newspaper. Which she couldn't be.

Her mind reeled with a memory of photographers and flashing bulbs. Had the paper published a picture of a disobedient girl forbidden to sing with her class? She pulled on her cotton kimono, her fingers fumbling.

When she pushed open the *fusuma* screen, she saw all the others leaning over a newspaper spread open on a table. Oki-sensei turned at once. "Tamura Chiyo, how did this happen?"

"This . . . what?" The satisfaction in Hoshi's face said the paper held bad news. Had something happened to one of the dolls? To Emily Grace? Was she cracked in her fall? *But she didn't fall. I caught her.*

As the others made room for her, the koi Chiyo had imagined lying dead in her stomach suddenly flicked its tail. Her own face filled most of the newspaper's upper half! She sank to her knees beside the low table. Above the picture, in quotation marks, were the words *"You are home."*

The picture showed her holding Emily Grace, looking directly into the doll's wide eyes. How trusting Emily Grace looked, as if she knew that Chiyo would take care of her.

I wish I could, Chiyo thought. Had such longing

been in her face when she held the doll? Such . . . tenderness? Everything she had felt at that moment was revealed. The photographer had caught it all.

"Miss Tamura," Sensei said severely, "you have disgraced yourself and the rest of us with you."

"Sumimasen." She stared unhappily at the photo, but nothing in it changed, no matter how hard she wished it would. This should have been a picture of the ambassador's daughter and the granddaughter of a shogun. Those girls were probably used to having their pictures shown in public. Everyone expected it of them. No one expected it of Tamura Chiyo.

The picture was all she would ever have of the doll who had captured her heart the moment she opened her blue eyes. Despite the humiliation, Chiyo wanted to keep the picture so that she could look at Emily Grace and wish her well.

It was best to say nothing now. *Sensei is too upset,* she warned herself. *She will probably rip the paper into pieces if she knows I want it.*

"Listen." Kimiko held up the paper. "Here's what they've written. 'The tenderness in this little girl's face speaks to the heart more poignantly than any words heard during yesterday's welcome.'"

"That one of our girls should be displayed in

the newspaper for anyone to look upon . . ." Sensei staggered backward to balance against a table. "Oh, I fear I will collapse!"

Kimiko said, "It goes on."

If only the floor would open up and stop her from reading, Chiyo thought. *This would be a very good time for a small earthquake to shake the country.*

Kimiko did not stop reading. "'When asked what she whispered to the doll called Emily Grace, Miss Tamura Chiyo answered, "You are home."'"

"Her name!" Oki-sensei fanned herself rapidly. "The newspaper used her name!"

Chiyo sank a little lower, as if every part of her grew smaller. When the photographer asked, she had blurted out her name as if his question must be answered. This was what careless thinking led to—disgrace. She would never be allowed to attend her sister's wedding.

Kimiko continued to read. "'You are home. What a simple phrase to put all the speeches to shame. This girl's warm heart speaks for all the Japanese girls who are embracing these beautiful dolls with their message of friendship.

"'When little Miss Tamura said to the doll, "Oh, how I hope you will come to my school," her entire heart was in her voice. Japan is filled with girls as loving as this, and we are awed and thankful for every one.'"

"How did he get your name?" Tomi asked.

Chiyo could only answer in deepening despair. "I told him."

"You told him!" Sensei sank onto a cushion, looking as if her legs would no longer hold her. "I will hear from Yamada-san. And from your parents. This is a disaster."

Hoshi said in a pitying tone, "She must go back to the country before she brings more shame to us all . . . for a doll she will never see again."

Chiyo pulled strength from the very center of her heart. "Wherever she goes, I hope she will be loved."

"Loving the dolls is the point of your picture, isn't it?" Kimiko asked, surprising her with approval. "All Japanese girls should open their hearts to the dolls, as you have done. Girls all over the country will see the truth of that."

"The newspaper said nice things," Hana added.

Shizuko said, "Perhaps it is not as bad as we first thought."

A knock sounded at the door. No one moved.

Then Shizuko hurried to answer. Watanabe-sensei rushed past her into the room, waving a folded note.

"The mayor of Tokyo has sent a message! He wishes to meet Miss Tamura Chiyo who, he has learned, represents Tsuchiura."

CHAPTER 21

Everyone spoke at once. "The mayor?"

"Why?"

"He wants to see Chiyo?"

"It's because of the picture!"

Oki-sensei simply moaned.

Hoshi slowly shook her head. "Poor Chiyo. I'm so sorry the newspaper used your picture in place of Miss Tokugawa's."

Watanabe-sensei said, "Ladies, please! Miss Tamura, you must get dressed at once. The mayor is sending his personal automobile for you in one hour."

Tomi and Shizuko said together, "His automobile!"

"He must wonder why the picture is not of Miss Tokugawa. Is our student to be officially reprimanded?" Oki-sensei snatched the newspaper from Kamiko, becoming again the teacher with her head full of schedules. "He cannot see her. Our train leaves in little more than an hour. We return home today."

"We will stay a day longer," Watanabe-sensei told her. "I have already arranged for the tickets to be changed. Listen, I will read the mayor's message."

He adjusted his glasses before reading solemnly, "'The honorable mayor of Tokyo requests the privilege of posing for a picture with Miss Tamura Chiyo, whose glowing love for the little doll ambassadors speaks eloquently for all Japanese girls.'"

Oki-sensei's voice rose nearly to a shriek. "He wants a picture with her?"

Hoshi put a hand to her mouth before saying, "Tsuchiura Girls' School will lose all respect."

"I disagree, Miss Miyamoto." Watanabe-sensei took the newspaper from Oki-sensei's limp hand and studied the photo. "The tenderness in Miss

Tamura's face as she looks at the doll speaks well for the young ladies of Tsuchiura Girls' School." He handed the paper to Kimiko. "Our school will be seen as encouraging compassion, and that is a good thing."

His gaze reached Hoshi. "Of course, our best efforts may not succeed with all our students."

Hoshi raised her chin. "Oki-sensei, I will spend the day in the shops. I need a new kimono jacket for the spring. There is nothing worth having in Tsuchiura."

Chiyo moved closer to Sensei as he placed the newspaper on a table. She slipped the paper into a fold of her robe when everyone was watching Hoshi. The newspaper must be saved. Her parents would not think the story shamed her.

"A day in the shops may be well spent," Oki-sensei agreed. "We will all go. The mayor has not requested our company."

"I will escort Miss Tamura." Watanabe-sensei turned to Chiyo. "Bathe! Dress! Comb your hair! Go! I will meet you downstairs. There is scarcely time for breakfast."

"There is no need for the rest of us to rush," Oki-sensei said. "Hurry downstairs for your bath,

Miss Tamura. Do not keep the mayor waiting. And try not to embarrass us further." The teacher looked around. "What has become of that wretched newspaper?"

Kimiko looked at the table. "It was right there."

Chiyo wanted to escape. She had just been told to hurry, but there was no choice. "I have it."

"You have it!" Oki-sensei's frown darkened her face.

Chiyo felt her own face burn with embarrassment. Once again, everyone was looking at her. "My parents will like to see it."

Oki-sensei shook her head. "I look at that picture and see a girl who picked up a doll against direct orders from her teacher. I also see a girl who sang when she had been told to remain silent." She looked hard at Chiyo. "Is that what you wish to share with your parents?"

Chiyo thought with a hollow feeling, *I look at my teacher and see someone who resents extra work caused by an untrained girl in her dance class. That must be why she is so cross.* Did Sensei also resent having a hill country girl in her class?

Chiyo turned, hoping Watanabe-sensei would understand why the paper was important to her, but he had already gone downstairs. "No," she answered Oki-sensei in a small voice.

"No." Sensei spoke in her no-nonsense classroom tone. "What appears in the newspaper today is forgotten tomorrow. We will not speak of this again and we will not keep old news."

She held out her hand. Blinking hard, Chiyo handed her the folded paper.

The teacher snatched it from her. "One of you please ask a maid to take away this trash. Miss Tamura, if you do not hurry, you will keep the mayor waiting, and that will not do."

Chiyo was glad to escape past the *fusuma* screen to gather her dark school uniform and stockings. After soaping and scrubbing in the bathing room of the hotel basement, she soaked briefly, then hurried into her clothes. As she combed her hair, her thoughts churned. She had not wanted her picture taken.

And she didn't want the mayor's attention or the car he was sending. Well . . . maybe the car. She had never dreamed she might ride in one. A shiver of excitement began in her toes and worked its way through her.

She could only hope that Yamada-san would not

hear of this and decide Masako's younger sister had drawn too much attention for him to wish to marry into her family. *After all,* Chiyo reassured herself, *if he had not sent me away from home, none of this would have happened.*

Downstairs, Watanabe-sensei rushed her through breakfast. It didn't matter. She was far too excited to eat. Soon she waited with Sensei in the hotel lobby, looking toward the street door each time it opened.

Sensei gave so much advice, her head swam. Don't be frightened. Behave naturally. Do not embarrass yourself or the school. She didn't mind the advice. She was glad he was going with her. Sensei would tell her the right things to say and do, things she hadn't had time to learn.

Fresh air rushed in with the opening door to the lobby. A man in a crisp blue jacket and cap asked, "Miss Tamura?"

Chiyo's heart leaped. Watanabe-sensei answered for her. "We are ready."

The mayor's automobile was long and black and even more elegant than others Chiyo had seen. With a flourish, the driver opened a back door. The car even smelled important. Feeling as if she had stepped into a dream, Chiyo settled inside next to the far window. A velvet curtain was drawn back, and she leaned closer to look out at the street.

In her own village, she had rarely ridden in an oxcart. Since leaving, she had traveled in a carriage behind Yamada-san's beautiful horse and ridden in rickshaws and that huge, noisy train. And now an automobile!

The uniformed man cranked a handle at the front of the car. When the engine rumbled to life, the entire vehicle vibrated. Chiyo vibrated along with it, but from excitement. Sensei sat properly still. She tried to copy him, though she wanted to bounce on the springy seat.

The driver hurried around and climbed behind the steering wheel. In moments, they were rolling smoothly into the street. Chiyo scarcely had time to look at people or into shop windows before they were gone and something even better came into view.

Or something worse. She began to notice posters in many shop windows, posters holding large copies of the newspaper photo. There she was on that corner. And in that window. And again, there!

When they paused at a corner, a young boy on

the street pointed through the window. "That's her! That's the girl! That's Chiyo!"

Several other boys ran with him as the car moved on, all of them shouting, "Chiyo-chan! Chiyo-chan!"

"Why are they shouting?" she exclaimed. "What do they want?"

"You have become a celebrity," Sensei answered. "They want to be close to you."

"I don't want to be a celebrity." What did that even mean? "I'm just a student. I'm nobody, Sensei. They are all mistaken."

"There is no mistake," he answered in a serious voice that told her she must listen. "You have become much more than you think, Miss Tamura. Now you must live up to what you have become."

CHAPTER 22

When the mayor's big car pulled to a stop in front of a large building, Chiyo clenched her hands in her lap. "Why does he want to see me?" she asked Watanabe-sensei, trying to keep her voice from shaking. "Do you think he is angry?"

What if Hoshi was right? The mayor might be upset that her picture had taken the place of one that should have been in the paper: a picture of Miss Tokugawa Yukiko. She almost expected to see the ghost of Yukiko's grandfather the shogun waiting with his sword drawn.

"You have struck a sympathetic chord in people's hearts," said Watanabe-sensei. "I believe that is why the mayor wishes to have his picture taken with you."

That didn't make sense to Chiyo. Hoshi was right. She was just a girl from a mountain village and always would be. Her cold fingers curled into her palms. "Do I have to meet him?"

Sensei nodded gravely. "Be proud, Miss Tamura. Remember, you are representing Tsuchiura Girls' School."

That didn't make her feel better. That made her feel worse. She did not want to represent Tsuchiura Girls' School to the mayor of Tokyo. She worried that every word escaping her lips would be the wrong one. Desperately, she asked, "What shall I say?"

Sensei smiled as the chauffeur opened the car door. "You'll know."

Chiyo drew in a deep, deep breath and stepped from the car. An aide greeted them with a bow before leading them through a hall busy with hurrying people. Many startled Chiyo by pausing to bow as she came near.

Wondering if they were mistaking her for someone important, she returned their bows. When the aide guided them through an open doorway, the mayor rose from behind a gleaming desk. He hurried forward to offer Watanabe-sensei a Western-style handshake.

Pleasure glowed in his eyes as he turned and bowed to Chiyo. "Welcome, Miss Tamura. Welcome! I am honored by your visit."

He wasn't angry, nor was the ghost of a shogun waiting with his sword. She breathed her thanks as she returned the bow. *"Arigatogozaimasu."*

"No, no," the mayor corrected. "You are the one who deserves gratitude, Miss Tamura. Through your picture, you have shown the world the warm, loving hearts of all Japanese children."

She bit her tongue to keep from blurting out that the picture was an accident, that she hadn't even known it was being taken. She cast a quick sidewise glance at Watanabe-sensei. Was she doing the right thing? *The Hoshi thing?* Sensei seemed satisfied with her. So far.

When the mayor invited them to sit down, she perched uneasily on the edge of a chair. Several photos on the walls showed the mayor posing with different people. Was her picture to go up there, posing with him?

She brought her gaze back quickly as he asked

about her home and family. Would he change his mind about a picture when he learned that she was just a girl from a mountain village?

The aide returned with two men, one with a large camera with a flash attachment. The mayor shook hands with both, then introduced Chiyo to the photographer, whom she remembered from the ceremony. The second man wrote for the paper that had published her picture.

She stood and bowed, unsure what was expected, but soon she was standing beside the mayor, watching the photographer adjust his camera. The writer made rapid notes on a pad in his hands.

"The exchange of dolls is the exchange of hearts," the mayor told him, sounding as if he expected to be quoted. "The glowing tenderness in Miss Tamura Chiyo's popular photograph has shown us that truth more clearly than any words spoken during the recent ceremony."

He moved closer to Chiyo. White light flashed. The photographer had taken their picture. For a long moment, Chiyo couldn't see anything but a bright glare.

The mayor seemed untroubled. She supposed he was used to camera flashes. "Miss Tamura," he said, facing her again, "I wish to appoint you to an important position. If you will accept, you will do our city a great honor."

She didn't know what to say. What was he asking her? What if she couldn't do it . . . whatever it was?

He motioned to his assistant, who stepped forward holding a doll with curly golden hair. When he handed the doll to the mayor, her eyelashes rolled open as if she were just waking. Her clear blue eyes looked directly at Chiyo. "Mama."

Chiyo gasped. "Emily Grace!"

"Miss Tamura," the mayor said, "with your permission, I hereby appoint you Honorary Protector of the doll Emily Grace."

As he handed the doll to her, the camera's flash lit up the room, but for Chiyo the camera had ceased to exist. Without conscious thought, she drew the doll close and gazed into her face. She had never expected to see Emily Grace again.

The mayor asked, "Miss Tamura, will you do the city the honor of accepting the appointment?"

For a moment, Chiyo couldn't speak at all. She looked from Sensei to the mayor through a blur of happy tears. "*Hai.*" She said it again with emphasis that made the watching men chuckle. "*Hai!* I would like that better than anything in the entire world!"

She swallowed hard, trying to blink away the haze of tears. "What does it mean, Honorary Protector?"

CHAPTER 23

The mayor smiled while the writer made more rapid notes. "I believe you will find the task pleasant, Miss Tamura. You see, I have arranged for Emily Grace to join the girls at your school. Your job will be to make her feel at home in Tsuchiura."

Again, Chiyo heard the reporter's pencil scratching against his notebook. "Our school?" She hardly dared believe it. "She's really coming to our school? Emily Grace?"

"She is." The mayor chuckled at her excitement. "Your heartwarming photograph convinced the committee members that Emily Grace should go to Tsuchiura."

He added to the writer, "Already this morning we have heard from many good people wanting to make sure the doll will be sent with Miss Tamura."

Chiyo pressed her cheek to Emily Grace's soft curls. Her heart filled with so many things she might say, but she could manage only "*Arigatogozaimasu!*"

The white flare came again. Another photograph. This time, she scarcely noticed. *Let him print it,* she thought. *Let it be my thank-you to all those kind people who want Emily Grace to go with me.*

"I promise," she said. "I will protect Emily Grace and keep her safe. If an earthquake comes, I will protect her with my own body!" She couldn't think of a bigger disaster that might threaten the doll—well, maybe Hoshi—but whatever came, she would save the doll before saving herself.

"Excellent!" The mayor reached into a box on his desk for a large medal. He read aloud the kanji characters printed in black ink across the front. "'Official Doll Protector by appointment of the Mayor of the City of Tokyo.'"

After displaying the medal to the reporter, he pinned it carefully to Chiyo's collar.

Blinking in still another white flash, Chiyo asked the doll softly, "Do you see this medal, Emily

Grace? This is a promise that I will always love you and keep you safe."

Her thoughts swirled. Was it only this morning that Oki-sensei and the other girls believed she was in serious trouble? She still didn't know how Yamada Nori would feel about the public attention.

She couldn't worry about that while Emily Grace was in her arms. The doll was to return with her to Tsuchiura! She had never been so happy in her life.

"Miss Tamura," the mayor said, "I hope you will be pleased to know that the medal comes with a cash gift."

He offered two gleaming gold coins. Chiyo accepted them, feeling numb with disbelief. *Ten yen. He was giving her two gold ten-yen coins!* "I . . . I don't know what to say. *Arigatogozaimasu,* Your Honor. *Arigatogozaimasu!*"

Tears slipped down her cheeks, but they were happy tears, and she smiled through them while the camera flashed again.

The mayor seemed in no hurry to end the meeting, but talked of the dolls and the ceremony the day before. "The doll called Miss America is to have a place of honor in the doll palace."

Doll palace? Chiyo looked at him, wishing to

know more. Fortunately, Watanabe-sensei asked for her. "There is to be a doll palace? I have not heard of that."

"Ah," said the mayor, sounding pleased. "I have the pleasure of being first to tell you the news. What do you think of this, Miss Tamura? Our empress has decided to donate a two-story doll palace large enough to hold the forty-eight dolls representing the forty-eight states of America, as well as the Miss America doll accepted by Miss Tokugawa and several Japanese doll assistants."

Chiyo thought of the dolls displayed before the welcoming ceremony and tried to imagine a doll palace large enough to hold forty-nine of them and more besides. "It will be very large."

"It will," the mayor agreed. "I understand our finest cabinetmaker is already working on the project. The forty-nine dolls will first visit the Imperial Palace. When the large dollhouse is completed in the Tokyo Educational Museum, they will all be moved there."

Chiyo wished she could see it, but the teachers weren't likely to bring the group all the way back to Tokyo from Tsuchiura to see a palace filled with dolls. She found it hard to believe she was here at all and not deep in a wonderful dream.

"There is one more thing to be decided." The mayor's eyes sparkled. "In appreciation of your kind heart, Miss Tamura, the city has arranged for you to visit Hirata Gouyou."

The name meant nothing to Chiyo. The mayor looked as if it should. She looked uneasily at Sensei as the mayor turned to him, saying, "Watanabe-sensei, you will recognize the name of a master doll maker. Hirata Gouyou is even now creating one of fifty-eight dolls to be sent to the children of America in gratitude for their kind gift to us. She will be called Miss Tokyo to represent our city."

The mayor turned to Chiyo. "Do you know of these dolls, Miss Tamura?"

She thought of Kaito-sensei telling the class about dolls to represent every prefecture and major city, big dolls the size of small children. Was she really to see one of those dolls—Miss Tokyo—being made? She knew that the glow she felt inside must be shining from her eyes.

When she saw the mayor exchange an amused glance with his aide, she found her voice. "*Hai*, honorable mayor. Sensei told us one hundred and fifty doll makers competed, hoping to be chosen to create the dolls."

"So they did," the mayor said with as much

approval as if she had managed a difficult word in a spelling contest. "Do you also know that our doll makers are able to make these exquisite dolls because the children of Japan have donated their own money to pay for them?"

"*Hai*, I was first in my class to donate a sen." Was that boastful? Should she have held her tongue? Worried, she glanced at Watanabe-sensei. He looked as pleased as the mayor, and she relaxed again.

"That does not surprise me." The mayor glanced at the reporter as if to make sure the man had heard her. Were all her comments going to appear in the paper? She pictured the scale she kept in her imagination. A picture in the newspaper weighed heavily on the *not humble enough* side. But now she had Emily Grace. Emily Grace weighed the other side of the scale.

The doll and medal mean I'm trusted, Chiyo told herself. *Keeping Emily Grace safe will prove to Yamada-san how responsible I've become.*

Trust and responsibility . . . those had to weigh more on the good side of the scale than keeping expression from her face or walking with tiny steps. She hugged the doll closer. *Taking care of Emily*

Grace will prove that I'm worthy enough to go home for Masako's wedding.

"You have only one more pleasant decision to make," the mayor told her, and she felt doubt prickle. What else could there be? "I understand six young ladies are here from Tsuchiura. You may invite any of them to visit the doll maker with you."

"Any of them?" If she took another of the girls, would that add to the good side of her imaginary scale? Who could she take? Hana, of course! But taking Hoshi might prove more to Yamada-san.

"Any of the girls," the mayor said cheerfully. "You probably have a special friend among them. Or take all, if you wish. Tell us, Miss Tamura. Who will explore Hirata Gouyou's doll-making studio with you?"

CHAPTER 24

Chiyo thought of the girls who were shopping today because they weren't invited to meet the mayor. Should she take them all?

How could she invite Hoshi, even to add good weight to that scale? She pictured Hoshi alone in the hotel, fuming while the others visited the doll maker. Maybe Hoshi would think before being mean to someone after that.

But she couldn't help remembering Hoshi's father scolding her for not being a good leader. What would he say if she was the only one not invited to the doll maker's workshop? Maybe he would say, *This is not the way of a leader*, making her feel less important than the smallest fish in the stream.

Chiyo didn't want to think of that because when she did, she imagined herself in Hoshi's place and how it must feel to have a father who demanded so much while showing no kindness.

"Well, Miss Tamura," the mayor asked again, sounding amused but a little impatient, "is the decision difficult? Who will you take with you?"

"All the girls," Chiyo said, hardly believing that she was including Miyamoto Hoshi. "I would like all six of us to go, please." She drew a quick breath. "And our two teachers, too."

"You are a young lady with a warm heart, as we already know." The mayor nodded toward his aide. "The arrangements will be made. Will tomorrow afternoon meet your approval?"

Chiyo looked quickly at Sensei, feeling all the plans collapse. "We've already stayed an extra day. We are to go home to Tsuchiura in the morning."

Sensei shook his head. "We will prolong our visit for yet another day."

How easily plans could be changed. At home, life moved on a schedule. If you did not feed the goat on time, there would be no milk and the goat would cry. But here, it seemed that plans changed easily and no one was even surprised.

When she returned to the hotel with Emily Grace in her arms, Chiyo felt as if she floated above the tatami. Maybe that was because Emily Grace seemed to float with her. "I'm so glad you're going home with me," she told the doll.

She was sure she saw the sweet smile widen.

"I wonder what Hoshi will say when she learns we will all visit the doll maker. What do you think, Emily Grace?" She bent her ear to the doll's lips. "Oh, you think she will say something nice? I hope you are right."

As she neared the room, she heard voices. The other girls were back from their shopping. She could hardly wait to tell them her news.

Hoshi was nearest when she opened the door from the hotel hall. Chiyo saw her crumple a newly purchased kimono jacket in her hands. "Is that . . . ? It is! It's that doll! You stole that doll!"

"No," Chiyo began, startled. It had never occurred to her that anyone would think she had just taken Emily Grace.

Hoshi tossed the jacket to a nearby cushion,

talking too fast for Chiyo to get in a word to explain. "Miss Tamura, I fear you've brought shame on our school!"

"You don't understand," Chiyo exclaimed, thinking maybe she wouldn't invite Hoshi to the doll maker's after all.

"Of course I do." Hoshi raised her voice. "Sensei, we have a problem with poor Miss Tamura. She has stolen that doll!"

"How could I steal her?" Chiyo was sorry she'd run ahead while Watanabe-sensei arranged with the hotel for another night. He would have cleared this up in a moment.

Oki-sensei rushed over with the other girls behind her. When she saw the doll, her mouth dropped open. "Oh! Oh . . . *oh*." She groped blindly for a table and balanced against it.

Doesn't she know me at all? Shock turned Chiyo's entire body cold. Never in her life had she taken something that didn't belong to her. Except maybe Hoshi's favorite chair that first day at school.

"Where is her crate?" Kimiko asked.

"And her suitcase and passport?" asked Shizuko.

Hana looked too stunned to say anything. Then she looked away.

They all think I've stolen Emily Grace! Even

Hana! Moments earlier, Chiyo had been looking forward to bringing Emily Grace to the hotel. This was her welcome? To be called a thief?

She was sure the imaginary koi in her stomach had not only sickened, but died. "Those things, the crate and the suitcase and everything, they've all been sent to the railroad station."

"You saw her crate ready to be shipped," Hoshi said, "and took her from it! Miss Tamura, you poor foolish girl."

Chiyo raised the medal pinned to her collar. "Do you think I stole this?"

Sensei peered at the medal and slowly read aloud, "'Official Doll Protector by appointment of the Mayor of the City of Tokyo.' Miss Tamura, what does this mean?"

"It means I promised to protect her and I will." Her earlier excitement rushed back and she exclaimed, "She's going to our school . . . to Tsuchiura!"

"But how could that happen?" Sensei asked. "If you didn't . . . just take her, how is it that you have her?"

The door was still open to the hallway. Watanabe-sensei stepped inside at last. "Have you told them the happy news, Miss Tamura?"

Chiyo turned to him in relief. "I tried. They don't believe me!"

He put one hand on her shoulder as if to share the respect everyone felt for him. "Then I am pleased to reassure all of you. Our Tamura Chiyo won the heart of the mayor of Tokyo. She has won the hearts of people everywhere!"

Oki-sensei looked even more confused. "What are you saying?"

"Just this! The mayor has been hearing from people who saw the picture in the newspaper. Everyone wants this doll to go to Miss Tamura's school. The mayor of Tokyo listens to the people, and he has arranged for Emily Grace to join us. Even better, Miss Tamura has been appointed the doll's protector."

He looked at Chiyo. "Have you shown them your medal?"

"*Hai.*" It felt good to see belief come slowly into Oki-sensei's eyes.

Yet envy in the other girls' faces didn't feel as satisfying as she'd expected. In her mind, *Okaasan* warned that boasting becomes sorrow when friends turn away. Chiyo decided not to tell them about the cash prize.

Still, she couldn't resist upsetting Oki-sensei

once more to pay her back for thinking she would steal Emily Grace. "My picture and my name will probably be in the newspaper again."

"They certainly will be," said Watanabe-sensei, as if announcing good news. "Our Chiyo made a great impression on the mayor. She represented the girls of Tsuchiura Girls' School with exceptional grace. We can now say . . . as the mayor does . . . that Tamura Chiyo represents all the girls of Japan."

Hoshi made a strangling sound. Chiyo enjoyed hearing it. "So you didn't need to worry," she told her astonished teacher, feeling a little spiteful.

"I . . . I am very glad to hear that," Oki-sensei said.

"I'm relieved to hear it." Hoshi's sarcasm showed she was not one bit sorry for having accused Chiyo of theft.

Tomi and Shizuko looked at each other before Tomi said, "We're proud of you, Chiyo. And the doll is coming to Tsuchiura! How wonderful!"

Hana gently touched Chiyo's hand. "I'm sorry I believed Hoshi, even for a moment."

"It's all right," Chiyo said. "I probably would have believed her, too." But she didn't think she would have believed Hoshi if the girl had accused Hana, not even for a moment.

She couldn't stay disappointed for long. Everyone wanted to hear about her meeting with the mayor, although Hoshi pretended to be bored. The rest of the girls gathered around to admire Emily Grace, her blue eyes, her golden curls. "It's real hair," Chiyo said. "Just feel it!"

"So soft," Shizuko marveled. "I wanted to touch one of the dolls when we saw them at the ceremony, but I didn't dare."

"Does she talk?" Tomi asked. "I've heard they do."

"Yes." Chiyo hesitated, then handed Emily Grace to the girl. "Lean her back and raise her up again."

"Mama," Emily Grace said obediently.

Chiyo explained, "That is her word for *okaasan.*"

The girls all exclaimed, "Ohh." Each wanted a turn holding the doll to make her talk. Chiyo watched, feeling proud but uneasy at letting Emily Grace out of her hands.

Hoshi handed the doll on to Kimiko. "I remember how much I enjoyed dolls when I was five years old."

"So now you are too old for dolls?" Chiyo asked.

Hoshi said, "I prefer books." Her tone said that anyone who preferred dolls was still a baby.

"Then you will not care to accompany us tomorrow."

Hoshi's perfect eyebrows lifted. "Accompany you where?"

"You wouldn't be interested. It's about dolls." Chiyo bent to straighten Emily Grace's collar, but she couldn't hold back her excitement. "We've all been invited to visit the doll maker who is working on a doll to send to America. She's called Miss Tokyo, to represent this city."

Kimiko clapped her hands, then paused. "You said 'all' of us. Do you mean . . . who do you mean?"

Watanabe-sensei beamed. "Miss Tamura has a generous heart. When the mayor asked who she would like to take with her, she asked that everyone be invited."

Chiyo looked from one to the other, pleased to see excitement in all their faces. Even Hoshi set aside the book she had just opened. "Imagine," Chiyo said. "The dolls are ninety centimeters tall, the size of a small child. Emily Grace and her friends are not even half that."

Hana bounced up and down, then stopped. "Aren't we going home tomorrow?"

Watanabe-sensei answered. "The tickets have been changed again."

Again! Throughout the afternoon and evening, Chiyo felt as if she were living inside a magic bubble where nothing was like her real world.

In her own space beyond the *fusuma* screen at last, Chiyo settled the doll between her futon and Hana's. Tomorrow, she would meet a master doll maker. Anticipation made her shiver, but gradually sleep overcame her as she lay with one hand curved protectively over Emily Grace.

CHAPTER 25

Chiyo woke early the next morning, too excited to sleep. She smoothed Emily Grace's hair before combing her own.

"Come downstairs for breakfast, girls," Oki-sensei called. "Chiyo, leave the doll here. You don't want to spill something on her."

I'm not that clumsy, Chiyo told herself. But she made sure Emily Grace was comfortable on a couch cushion before hurrying after the others.

She had expected General Miyamoto to join them for dinner the night before. He hadn't come by even though Hoshi kept glancing at the doorway.

When he came into the breakfast house soon after they were all seated, Chiyo looked for Hoshi and was surprised not to see her.

The girl rushed in moments later, bowed to her father, and found a seat at the table.

General Miyamoto was a nice-looking man, Chiyo thought after a modest glance. But his expression concealed whatever he might be thinking or feeling.

He stood beside an empty chair at the head of the table to greet them. "Breakfast this morning is my treat. I hope you will enjoy the omelets."

"What is an omelet?" Chiyo whispered to Hana. Hana didn't know, either. When they were served Western-style eggs, whipped, cooked quickly in butter—butter!—and folded over, they glanced from their plates to each other. Eggs were rarely eaten in Chiyo's family, since they sold what they could. And they never had anything cooked in butter.

While Hana poked curiously at her omelet, General Miyamoto looked down the table to Chiyo. "Miss Tamura, I have been hearing interesting things about you."

"Her picture is everywhere," Hoshi said, sounding as if she were proud of her classmate. Chiyo noticed that she was not the only one to look at Hoshi in surprise.

"*Hai*," Watanabe-sensei agreed. "Miss Tamura's picture has captured the heart of Japan."

The severe lines in General Miyamoto's face relaxed slightly. "Not often does a girl come from a mountain village and earn such wide approval."

Hoshi's mouth turned down, but she kept her thoughts to herself. Chiyo had noticed that while the general had nodded in return to her bow, he paid little attention to his daughter.

Hana exclaimed, "Chiyo met the mayor."

Both teachers looked sharply at Hana for speaking without invitation as the general asked, "Did you enjoy that meeting, Miss Tamura?"

"*Hai*. I rode in his car. It's very big and black and . . . rumbly." Was that a word? She felt heat in her face and wondered if her ears had turned red with embarrassment.

"And now," Hana said, still too excited to wait her turn to speak, "we are all to meet a doll maker who is making a huge doll to send to America."

Oki-sensei turned a forbidding look on Hana, who was forgetting her manners.

Hana murmured, "*Sumimasen*."

The general's eyes showed amusement. "Miss Nakata is the daughter of a politician," he reminded Sensei. "Words come easily." He turned to Chiyo. "Are you looking forward to the visit?"

"*Hai.*" She added impulsively, "Would you like to come with us, Miyamoto-san? Our teachers are going." At once, she realized that she shouldn't have asked. The others might not like having the general with them.

"*Arigatogozaimasu*, Miss Tamura," he answered. "As much as I would enjoy accompanying the group, I'm afraid an appointment elsewhere makes it impossible."

"Dolls?" Hoshi asked, looking at her father with disbelief breaking her usual composure. "You would visit dolls, *Otousama*?"

"Our Japanese dolls carry our history," he said with a glance around the table. "They tell the story of our people, from the little cylindrical *kokeshi* dolls the farmers' daughters enjoy to the larger ambassador dolls you will be meeting today."

As Chiyo thought of Momo, left behind at school to prevent charcoal from smearing her uniform, Hana said, "I have a *kokeshi* doll. I wonder why they are not made with arms or legs."

Oki-sensei gave her a *You have not been asked to speak* look but answered anyway. "Cylindrical dolls with ball heads are less expensive to make."

"There is beauty in simplicity," General Miyamoto said. "Each hand-painted face on a *kokeshi* is individual in its way, though the dolls may be very similar."

Chiyo glanced at Hoshi and saw a storm in her eyes, although she kept her expression calm. She was not thinking of Momo. Her anger said she did not like sharing her father's attention.

After a rickshaw tour of several shrines and lunch in a noodle house, they climbed into rickshaws again to ride to the doll maker's home studio in the heart of the city. As they traveled, Oki-sensei pointed out the drifting fragrance of newly blooming peach trees. "A good sign," Sensei said firmly. "Peach blossoms indicate serenity and gentle manners, traits very proper for young ladies."

"Breathe deeply," Chiyo whispered to Hana. "Then you will become proper."

Hana giggled. "That's all it takes? Breathing? I can do that!" She made such a show of inhaling deeply, she began to cough.

Chiyo teased, "You're as allergic to serenity as the flappers we saw that first day."

Hana put a hand over her mouth to cover a smile, but amusement sparkled from her bright eyes. They both knew what Sensei thought of flappers.

The rickshaws clattered across a bridge Chiyo recognized. They were near the railroad station. She couldn't help mentally following the rails back to Tsuchiura and the road home.

In the mountains, it would be colder than here where the land was so much lower, but *Otousan* would be preparing to plant his field. Longing ached through her. She should be there, helping.

Hana laughed suddenly at two dogs playing in the street, and the moment of sadness slipped away. Chiyo laughed with her for the excitement ahead, for the perfumed air carrying serenity, and for two dogs chasing each other.

Old houses lined one side of the street now. *Grandparents,* Chiyo thought, *settled comfortably while watching the high stone walls of modern buildings grow like ambitious children across the way.*

The rickshaw bearers came to a stop before an older house that looked dark and mysterious. Aged wood creaked with a rising wind that signaled coming rain. The roof of the doll maker's house sloped down on each side of shuttered windows.

While the teachers spoke with the rickshaw bearers, Chiyo and the others stepped onto a flat gray stone stretching to the front door. Eagerness had pushed Chiyo ahead, but now she stopped, suddenly shy.

"Ring the bell," Hana urged from just behind her.

He may be as severe a man as General Miyamoto, Chiyo told herself, edging back. "You ring it."

CHAPTER 26

Hoshi nudged her forward. "Ring the bell, girl-who-met-the-mayor."

Chiyo stumbled and flung one hand out for balance. Her fingers hit the bell.

"Your manners!" Oki-sensei protested just as the door slid open. A woman looked out at them, her brows coming together in a frown.

Watanabe-sensei stepped past the others. "Here are Tamura Chiyo and her friends from Tsuchiura Girls' School. The mayor arranged for them to meet with Hirata-san."

The woman made no move to let them pass. "I am Mrs. Sasaki, his housekeeper. You understand he is a busy man."

Hana whispered to Chiyo, "Step forward. Let her know you will not apologize or leave."

Chiyo shook her head, wishing she were anywhere else.

Sensei spoke in a firm tone he might use with a reluctant student. "These girls have come a long way."

The woman's frown deepened. "Hirata-san is very busy, but he is kind and has set aside his important work to spare a few minutes." Stepping back into a polished entry hall, she waited, radiating displeasure over the interruption of their visit while the girls quickly removed their shoes and set them to one side.

After snapping open an elegant *fusuma* screen, Mrs. Sasaki motioned the group to follow.

"She is proud of him," Chiyo whispered to Hana, "but she worries about him, too."

Hana whispered back, "She is his oni."

Chiyo giggled, agreeing. "*Hai*, his gatekeeper demon."

They hurried in their stockings after the woman, hushed by her disapproval. Chiyo glanced at painted *fusuma* screens as mysterious as lids to treasure boxes. Did the rooms beyond hold beautiful dolls in elaborate kimonos?

A second doorway opened into a workshop. Parts of dolls crowded shelves and tabletops and hung from hooks. One table held a clutter of small jars surrounded by colorful spatters of paint. Brushes of different sizes crowded other jars.

A man much younger than *Otousan* rose from a stool. Wood chips, chisels, and unfinished doll heads waited on a workbench beside him. Nothing like the severe artist Chiyo had expected, he looked as dashing as a samurai, with thick dark hair and dark eyes. Instead of a warrior's protective gear, he wore a paint-spattered apron over a soft tunic and trousers. "Come in, come in," he greeted them, smiling. "You are welcome, all of you!"

As they returned his bow, he asked the teachers, "Now, which is the girl from the picture I see posted everywhere?" His glance reached Chiyo and his smile deepened. "Ah, yes. I am honored to welcome you, Miss Tamura." He bowed again, especially for her.

Feeling clumsy over being singled out, Chiyo returned the bow. She was keenly aware of the other girls watching, especially Hoshi.

"You have all seen the dolls from America?" he asked. "You are fortunate. I have not yet had that pleasure."

Hana spoke despite a warning gesture from Oki-sensei. "Chiyo has one of them. We all held her. She says 'Mama.'"

"She is not mine, Hirata-san," Chiyo said, quick to explain. "The mayor arranged for Emily Grace to go to our school. I am to keep her safe."

"Emily Grace is the doll photographed with you? So she is to go to your school." He nodded approval. "Our mayor has made a wise decision."

When he took them around the workshop, explaining his various tools and their uses, Chiyo looked curiously at a bin filled with rough oyster shells. The doll maker was quick to notice her interest. He seemed often to be studying her.

"You are wondering what oysters have to do with doll making, Miss Tamura? There is magic here. When the oyster shell has been ground into powder with other materials and properly colored, it becomes *gofun*, a coating I will paint in many layers over the doll's face, hands, and feet."

He picked up a smaller finished doll and pointed out the pale coloring of her face. "Here you see the oyster shell has become the doll's natural-looking skin."

To Chiyo, the doll could not have looked more delicate if the entire head were made of china.

Imagine rough oyster shells becoming the smooth skin of a doll!

The doll maker turned to the high table where he had been working when they came in. An electric lantern cast a bright glow over a block of wood shaped vaguely like the head of a young child. "As you see, I have only blocked out the head. I have been looking for the right expression to carve into the doll to become Miss Tokyo."

They were all disappointed to learn that the doll was not yet finished, but the doll maker let them hold her hands, already carved of light wood.

"They even have dimples over their knuckles," Hana marveled.

Shizuko held up a doll hand. "Look! Perfect little fingernails!"

"When they are finished and covered in flesh-tinted *gofun*," the doll maker told them, "the hands will look so real you will think the fingers might curl around your own."

"What will she wear, Hirata-san?" asked Kimiko.

The doll maker removed a length of rose-colored silk from a cabinet. When he unfolded the material, they saw a kimono that might fit a small child. "The imperial dressmaker selected the fabric," he explained. "Do you see the hand-painted lotus blossoms? Designs chosen for each of the doll's kimonos must be suited for her smaller size."

He reached into the cabinet again for a brocade obi, along with a rope-like *obi-jime* to tie around the obi and hold the large bow in place at the back.

When they had admired those, the doll maker invited each of them to choose a *kokeshi* doll from a bin. Even Hoshi looked with interest at the little cylindrical figures with their ball-shaped heads. Although Hoshi's smile was as rare as her father's, one appeared briefly.

Chiyo wondered if she had already forgotten Momo and the gardener's fire.

"Many accessories will travel with Miss Tokyo," the doll maker told them. "She is to have a large round box to hold her tea sets and a long one filled with other items she will need."

He turned to the girls, his eyes lighting up. "Perhaps you can help me. Suppose Miss Tokyo was your little sister. Besides tea sets, small tables, and lanterns, what would you send along for her comfort?"

"Dolls," Hana said at once.

Chiyo agreed. "She should have a small doll of her own to keep her company. She can talk of home and the doll will understand, even when she's sad."

"Especially when she's sad," Hana said.

"Two dolls," Kimiko suggested. "She should take a boy and a girl doll to show to the American children."

"Worthy ideas." The doll maker opened a tall cabinet with several finished smaller dolls on the shelves. "I will be pleased to have you decide which two dolls should travel to America with Miss Tokyo."

To Chiyo, accustomed to small *kokeshi* dolls, those in the cabinet were like living children, with gentle faces and serene expressions. "Their hair looks real," she said.

The doll maker chuckled. "Their wigs are made of human hair. Miss Tokyo will have natural hair as well."

Calm brown glass eyes with painted lower lashes and brush-stroked eyebrows on the nearest doll made Chiyo feel as if the doll gazed back at her with a soft smile curving her lips. "She is perfect," she murmured, and felt a twinge of guilt, as if her comment betrayed Emily Grace.

"*Arigatogozaimasu*, Miss Tamura. As with any doll artist, I try to understand the heart of each doll I create. This helps me paint her expression in a way that will bring her to life for her young owner."

He said to the two teachers, "As I mentioned before, I have been searching for the look that will be right for Miss Tokyo. I have found it." He turned to Chiyo. "Miss Tamura, will you honor me by posing for several sketches? I will use them later as guides to help me complete the doll."

CHAPTER 27

Hirata Gouyou wanted to put her face on Miss Tokyo! Chiyo nodded, too astonished to speak.

"*Hai.* It will be so," the doll maker exclaimed. "Mrs. Sasaki, when the young ladies have chosen the two dolls to travel with Miss Tokyo, please direct them to the garden, where they may enjoy a cup of tea."

He beamed at the teachers. "I have been searching for a subtle sweetness of expression for this doll. It is difficult to explain in words, but I knew I would recognize it when I saw it."

"In Miss Tamura?" Oki-sensei asked, as if unable to believe such a thing.

"*Hai.* At last, I have found the model I need." The artist gazed at Chiyo. "The doll must have a glow of inner strength and yet show the gentleness we see in our Japanese girls."

He studied Chiyo as if memorizing the curve of her cheek and the shape of her eyes. "I see those qualities in Tamura Chiyo. Her face will become Miss Tokyo."

Watanabe-sensei smiled. "What do you think of a doll that looks like you traveling to America, Miss Tamura?"

She was too stunned to know. Once again, she was being set apart. The other girls looked at her as if she were a stranger. She had tried hard to fit in, to become one of them.

Even Oki-sensei was smiling now. Both teachers looked as proud of her as if they had brought her here for this honor that did not feel like an honor when she looked at her friends.

She didn't want to disappoint the kind doll maker. "Since I cannot go to America," she said at last, "I am glad the doll will go for me and ask the American girls to be our friends."

Hoshi turned to Kimiko and muttered just

loudly enough to be heard, "Does she lie awake at night thinking of speeches?"

Chiyo wanted to ask, *Isn't that expected of a leader?* She remained quiet. This was not the time to argue with Hoshi.

"Girls," Oki-sensei warned those still at the doll cabinet, "hands off, please. Admire only with your eyes."

"No, no," Hirata-san corrected her. "They may touch the dolls. Pick them up if you like, young ladies. Hold them. Decide among you which should travel to America."

Chiyo longed to lift and admire the dolls from the cabinet. Instead she climbed onto a high stool the doll maker indicated and turned her face into the strong light of the electric lantern.

He sat nearby with a sketchbook, brush, and ink pot, and worked in swift, sure strokes. She hoped he would finish soon, but after the first few minutes, he flipped the page of his sketchbook, chose another angle, and began again.

"Do not look at your friends," he suggested gently. "A worried look is not what I want. Think of the girls in America the doll will meet."

Chiyo chose instead to think of finding Emily Grace and of how the doll had opened her long-lashed blue eyes and looked straight at her. Even so, posing soon became boring. She would much rather be with the other girls.

Kimiko held a boy doll in wide, loose trousers and a tunic. *He should go,* Chiyo decided, as if she had been asked. *But which of the girl dolls?* Hana and three others each held a doll and were trying to decide which was best.

Hoshi's assured voice argued for her choice. Chiyo thought silently, *She tries to lead, but she only knows how to be bossy.*

It was hard to sit still, away from the others, when she wanted to help decide which doll should make the journey. *It doesn't matter,* she told herself. *Any of those dolls will please the girls in America. They are all perfect.*

The doll maker's brush moved rapidly over the page, his expression intent. He was a master, and it was an honor to be sketched by him. But his brush paused. Had she frowned? She quickly returned her thoughts to Emily Grace. As the doll's blue eyes and sweet smile rose into her mind, she felt her face relax.

At last, the artist said that she might leave the stool. He removed the first page of his sketchbook and in deft strokes signed the characters that formed his name.

He offered the page to Chiyo. "I will be honored if you will accept this small sketch with my gratitude for your patience, Miss Tamura." Amusement warmed his eyes as they met hers. "Someday, a sketch bearing my signature may have value."

Chiyo gazed at the drawing in wonder. The artist had captured her so perfectly, she looked as if she might step off the page.

"*Arigatogozaimasu*," she said, bowing. "This picture will have a place of honor in my parents' home."

This single sketch meant far more than the posters showing her image throughout the city. She rolled it carefully so it would not become creased and placed it in a deep pocket in her skirt.

Mrs. Sasaki had taken the other girls and their teachers into the garden. Chiyo joined them in an open pavilion overlooking white sand raked in flowing waves around large black stones.

Oki-sensei was explaining that the peaks of raised sand represented the sea surging toward the large stone islands. Chiyo sank onto a cushion nearby and gazed out at the tranquil garden. For a moment, everything seemed right. Then she met a look from Hoshi that made her thankful the sketch was out of sight.

The doll maker joined them, settling comfortably on a cushion and accepting a cup of green tea. "Well, young ladies, have you decided which two dolls should travel to America with Miss Tokyo?"

Tomi and Shizuko said almost together, "*Hai!* The boy doll! We all agree."

With a glance at Hoshi, Kimiko said, "We haven't decided which of the girl dolls to send."

Hoshi looked at her with patience. "The doll with her lips parted so we see her teeth is the perfect choice."

Hana surprised Chiyo by objecting, since she rarely spoke back to Hoshi. "Most of us don't go around with our mouths open and our teeth showing. We should send the doll with closed lips tilted in the hint of a smile."

"The doll is to represent us," Tomi agreed.

"No," Hoshi said. "The doll with a secret smile does not represent me. Chiyo wears that smile at this very moment!"

Chiyo wondered if she did have a secretive smile on her lips. The drawing was like a hidden treasure in her pocket. She kept touching it to be sure it was still there. As much as she longed to show it to the others, she was afraid they would resent her more.

Opening her mouth to show her teeth, she asked Hoshi from behind them, "Is this better?"

The others laughed while Hoshi raised her eyebrows. "Be silly if you like. It changes nothing. The doll with parted lips is a leader. We must send the doll who looks ready to speak."

The artist said, "We will take a vote. I understand that is the American way. How better for our doll to begin her journey?"

"*Hai*," Watanabe-sensei agreed. "A vote is an excellent idea."

The girls nodded, although Hoshi looked away. She knew how a vote would go. She was right. Everyone, including Chiyo, voted to send the doll with the closed lips and soft smile.

They talked again of accessories to send with Miss Tokyo. Chiyo noticed Mrs. Sasaki hovering in a doorway like a storm cloud ready to end the party. Her expression warned that the artist might have to work late into the night to make up time lost to this visit.

Oki-sensei must have noticed, too. She brought the laughter and talk to an end. Thanking the artist for generously sharing his afternoon, she said, "We must return to the hotel now and pack. Our train will leave early in the morning."

Chiyo could hardly wait to be back with Emily Grace. She wished they were leaving right this minute. Soon afterward, when rickshaws had returned them to the hotel, she rushed ahead of the others to the doll.

The cushion where she had left Emily Grace was empty.

CHAPTER 28

Chiyo whirled to face the others as they came into the room. "Emily Grace! She's gone!"

Oki-sensei glanced about. "Where did you leave her?"

"There!" Chiyo pointed to the empty pillow on the couch. A dent still showed where she had pressed the doll against it. "But she's gone."

"She has to be here," Tomi said. "We're to take her with us."

Hoshi looked at Chiyo with pity. "Miss Tamura, how awful for you! People will be shocked to learn our school's doll disappeared while in the care of a simple farm girl."

"She has probably slipped behind something," Kimiko said, moving the pillows around on the couch.

Shizuko suggested, "The maids may have moved her while cleaning."

As everyone began to search, Hana leaned close to whisper, "Did you notice Hoshi came to breakfast after the rest of us?"

Chiyo nodded. She had to think like Hoshi. Where would she take the doll if she had only a few minutes?

She stepped into the hallway and looked in either direction. There were a few pairs of shoes left before closed doors, but they were only large enough to hide a *kokeshi.*

An anguished whisper came from the stairs. "Miss!"

The young maid Hoshi had scolded for bringing towels peeked from the stairwell.

"Hello," Chiyo said softly. "Um . . . Toyama?"

The girl looked around nervously. "Please come." She hurried to the far end of the hall and pointed to a tall ornamental vase standing below the window. "She is in there. The *ningyo.*"

"She's in there?" Chiyo stood on her toes to peer

into the vase. She could see the top of Emily Grace's blond curls. The doll was pushed deep inside. When Chiyo reached in, she felt the doll's pretty blue bow. If she pulled and it came off, the doll might slip deeper.

Pressing her cheek hard against the vase rim, she stretched even higher on her toes. Her fingers stretched past the curls to the doll's chin. Carefully, she pulled her out and into her arms.

"Emily Grace! Are you all right?" As she straightened the doll's dress and bow, Hana came from the room. "You found her!"

Toyama twisted her hands together. "I cannot accuse the other girl. Do you understand?"

"You saw who put her in there?" Hana asked.

Chiyo said quickly, "We understand. Don't worry, Toyama. We won't mention your name. You were kind to risk telling me. Hoshi would have accused you of hiding her in the vase."

"But . . ." Hana began, and fell silent. The maid's job could be in danger if she reported what she had seen.

Toyama said with more spirit, "You were kind to me. That other was not." Looking nervous again, she hurried away.

"*Arigatogozaimasu,*" Chiyo called after her. Cradling Emily Grace as if she were a lost child, she walked back to the room with Hana.

"We have her," Hana called.

All the girls crowded around, asking questions. Chiyo broke in. "She was inside the big vase at the end of the hall."

Even Oki-sensei looked at Hoshi.

Hoshi's eyebrows curved upward. "We should question the maid. She must have put it in there."

Hana rolled her eyes. "Why would she do that?"

"Isn't it obvious?" Hoshi sighed. "The poor girl has probably never owned a pretty doll. She meant to take it home with her once we stopped searching."

"The maid did not take Emily Grace," Chiyo said. "And I will not let our doll out of my sight again."

"That would be best," Oki-sensei said. "The emperor has welcomed the dolls. For Tsuchiura School to lose one entrusted to us would be deeply shameful."

Again, everyone looked at Hoshi. Hoshi looked at Chiyo and said gently, "Don't worry, Sensei. We will all see that Miss Tamura is more careful in the future."

• • •

After boarding the early morning train at the Tokyo station, Chiyo lifted Emily Grace to the window beside her seat. As they traveled, she pointed out passing sights. "See the houses with thatched roofs? My home is like that."

Hana spoke for the doll in a high-pitched voice. "What are those big animals?"

"Those are oxen," Chiyo answered, as if Emily Grace had really spoken. "See how patiently they plod along the road. Riding in a wagon pulled by oxen is much slower than the train."

"And smellier," Hana said, giggling.

Wheels clacked, the car swayed, and the whistle blew in long, haunting calls. After leaving Tokyo, they crossed the river Edo and later the river Tone, both crowded with flat-bottomed boats, rowing boats, and several steamers.

Small villages lay beside the river crossings. The train stopped at each to let off passengers and take on others. The village of Toride was celebrating a local festival. When the train paused, Chiyo waved the doll's arm at people in bright costumes and grinned when they waved back.

As they rolled along the tracks again with the wheels clacking a rhythm on the rails, Chiyo began to feel sleepy. Emily Grace lay back in her arms with her eyes closed. She was sleepy, too, Chiyo decided, and lay the doll on the seat.

Beside her, Hana played with her new *kokeshi*. "I will tell my doll at home this is her little sister. Her name is Miki." She leaned over to speak to Emily Grace. "That means beautiful princess."

Chiyo leaned Emily Grace forward and back. The doll said, "Mama."

Both girls laughed as Hana corrected, "Not 'Mama,' say 'princess.'"

Still smiling, Chiyo realized that even the train no longer seemed strange to her. "Hana, do you think we have changed?"

"What do you mean?"

"*Okaasan* said I must go to school and learn to change because Japan is changing. Have we changed?"

Hana looked as if trying to decide. "Does your *Okaasan* want you to become bold like a flapper?"

"No!"

"Does she want you to smoke cigarettes?"

Chiyo pressed a forbidding hand over her mouth. *Okaasan* would not let her leave the house for a month if she even thought of it. "No."

"Does she want you to stare at people who pass by, even strangers?"

"No, I have not changed."

"Yet you have become the face of all Japanese girls."

That thought made Chiyo uneasy. "The newspaper and the doll artist liked me because I look like a traditional Japanese girl." Relief made her smile. "I have not changed. I am traditional! Has school changed you, Hana?"

Hana considered the question. "*Hai.*"

"It has?" Chiyo looked at her friend in surprise. "How?"

"I was afraid of Hoshi. Now I'm not."

"I'm not afraid of her, either. I'm sorry for her a little." Chiyo held her forefinger and thumb a quarter inch apart. "I'm sorry this much."

Hana held her thumb and forefinger pressed together so tightly the tips turned white. "I'm sorry for her, too. This much."

They giggled together, but Chiyo glanced over the back of the seat and was glad to see Hoshi talking with Shizuko across the aisle and not listening to them.

She held Emily Grace to the window again to see small shrines. The ground had begun to rise toward tree-covered hills. When she pressed close to the window, she could see the peak of

Mount Tsukuba even farther north than her village home.

She reached into her pocket for her new *kokeshi* and felt the rolled artist's sketch. She had scarcely had a chance to look at it. With a glance at Hana, who had her eyes closed, she pulled it out and unrolled it.

"What is that?" Hana asked, awake after all. She leaned across Emily Grace. "Why, it's you, Chiyo! Sensei, look at this!"

CHAPTER 29

"Hirata-san made a lot of drawings," Chiyo said. "He gave me this for posing for him."

"It's very good." Hana took the drawing from her and called again to Oki-sensei. "Look, Sensei, the doll maker gave Chiyo one of his sketches."

Chiyo almost grabbed for the paper, but Hana was already handing it across the aisle to their teacher.

"It is very like you, Miss Tamura," Sensei said. "He has even signed the bottom."

The door at the front of the car opened with a whoosh of cooler air. The conductor came through, checking people's tickets. Everyone bustled a bit, searching through pockets or bags.

"My parents will like it," Chiyo told Sensei. "They'll put it in our alcove with flowers or budding tree branches."

"Like a spring scroll," Hana said.

"*Hai*," Sensei agreed. "Youth and spring are much alike."

Watanabe-sensei, sitting behind her, asked to see the picture. Oki-sensei handed it back to him while she reached into her bag for her ticket.

He studied the drawing, looking thoughtful. "Hirata Gouyou is one of Japan's finest doll makers, as was his father. Treasure this drawing, Miss Tamura."

"I will." Chiyo leaned across Hana to reach for it, but Hoshi, sitting behind the music teacher, asked to see the drawing. The conductor came closer, and Watanabe-sensei handed the picture to Hoshi while he located his ticket.

Feeling uneasy, Chiyo asked, "May I have the picture?"

Hoshi leaned forward as if to hand the drawing to Chiyo. The paper left her fingers and floated into the aisle. "Oops."

"Pick it up at once," Oki-sensei exclaimed.

Chiyo scrambled across Emily Grace and Hana to get into the aisle. But the conductor moved ahead, taking up most of the space. "Hoshi!" Chiyo exclaimed around him. "Grab it!"

Hoshi didn't move. The conductor, paying no attention to them, started toward the next row of seats. Chiyo felt her heart leap into her throat. "Stop! Please, stop!"

Around her, the world seemed to slow down. The conductor was laughing with someone over a comment they'd made. Chiyo watched in horror as his foot hovered over her picture.

"Don't step down. Please!"

For a moment, the car seemed frozen, with Watanabe-sensei starting to his feet. The conductor's foot hovered . . . then drew away. He bent down and picked up the picture, looking from the drawing to Chiyo. "Why, this is you, young lady. Anyone would see that right away. Who is the artist?"

"He's a doll maker," Chiyo said, hardly able to get words past a thickening in her throat.

"Yes," the conductor said. "Hirata Gouyou. I see his name here. And he has drawn you! Are you someone important?"

"No." Chiyo wished he would stop calling attention to her and give her the picture.

Hana said, "Yes, she is! The doll maker is going to put her face on a doll to represent all of Tokyo!"

The conductor's brows rose. "That is an honor! Young lady, you must take better care of this drawing."

"I will," Chiyo promised as he handed it to her. She added fiercely to herself, *I will never let it out of my hands again!*

The conductor moved on, and Hoshi said, "Poor Miss Tamura. Did you really think I would leave it there? It was a joke!"

Hana said, "Jokes are supposed to be funny."

Oki-sensei added, "Miss Miyamoto, of course you mean to apologize."

Hoshi sighed and said, "I am sorry Chiyo couldn't see the humor."

Chiyo thought, *That's not an apology. I don't have to accept it.*

Sensei said with a tight expression, "Has the drawing been harmed, Miss Tamura?"

"No," Chiyo answered, looking carefully at both sides of the paper.

"Then we will speak no more of it."

The incident might have been closed to the rest of them, the way the incident on the train platform was closed and the incident with the vase, but none were closed for Chiyo. She said low-voiced to Hana, "I don't even want to walk like her anymore. I'd rather stomp than glide like Hoshi."

Hana agreed. "Sometimes stomping is best."

After returning the sketch safely to her pocket, Chiyo lifted Emily Grace into her lap and straightened her skirt and collar. The train rolled ahead. Wheels clacked out a rhythm on the rails, and gradually she relaxed.

They passed more farms with thatch-roofed homes and outbuildings. The scenery began to look familiar. "We are almost home, Emily Grace," she said, lifting the doll to the window. "You will like the lake, and you might see the ruins of the old castle where a shogun once lived."

Hana grinned. "In Tsuchiura, little changes except for an old castle settling into the mud."

"Here, a schoolgirl is just a schoolgirl," Chiyo added with relief. "Someone no one ever notices."

Hana held her *kokeshi* toward the window. "Miki, welcome to boring Tsuchiura." The train lurched, and the doll slipped from her hand and rolled into the aisle. Hana scrambled after it and accidentally knocked it farther away "Shizuko, my doll went under your seat."

"I'll get it," Shizuko promised, bobbing below the seat back.

Chiyo watched Hana scramble to join her and smiled, thankful to be back in Tsuchiura. She held Emily Grace to the window again. "There's the station. And *Otousan* and *Okaasan*! They're with Yamada Nori! They've all come to meet the train."

She hugged the doll. "Maybe they've come to take me home!"

Throughout the train, everyone was gathering belongings, preparing to leave. Chiyo edged around Hana and Shizuko, still on their knees hunting for the *kokeshi*. Holding Emily Grace close, she moved past Hoshi and Kimiko, who were sorting out their packages. She was first of their group to step onto the platform at the back of the car.

Astonishment held her there.

CHAPTER 30

The station was full of people, even the headmaster. Bright banners fluttered over the platform. Someone was playing a flute, another, a drum. A group of students from Tsuchiura Girls' School began to sing the welcome song.

Headmaster Hanarai came forward. "Here is our doll ambassador," he announced. "We are all eager to welcome the little traveler from across the sea."

As she stood in the doorway of the railcar, holding the doll she had brought safely all the way from Tokyo, Chiyo felt as though she had won a difficult race. Before bowing politely to the waiting people, she lifted a hand in a tiny wave just for her parents, a wave that said *I see you and I love you and I can't wait to be with you.*

Watanabe-sensei urged her forward. "Take the doll to Headmaster Hanarai, Miss Tamura. Everyone is waiting to meet her."

Chiyo felt as if pulled between two countries, like Emily Grace. The warm country of family and childhood pulled her one way. The new country of her school pulled another.

Behind her, Sensei murmured, "You must officially hand over the doll."

Chiyo hesitated. She had loved Emily Grace and cared for her and kept her safe. Could she hand her away as if she were just some package brought from Tokyo?

Behind her, Hoshi muffled a laugh. *Hoshi thinks I won't let the doll go.* The uncertainty that had kept her on the small platform broke at the thought. As she crossed to the headmaster, she wondered what she should say. No one had told her. Did they expect her just to know?

Headmaster Hanarai bowed when she reached him. She was surprised, expecting to bow first to him. Quickly, she bowed in return and offered him the Friendship Doll, who now belonged to the school.

Words flowed from her heart. "Headmaster-san, here is Emily Grace. She has traveled all the way from America to bring the good wishes of American children."

Approval showed in his face as he answered. "The students and staff of Tsuchiura Girls' School are honored to welcome the little ambassador."

The gathered people seemed to expect more. They all looked at Chiyo. What else could she say? Lexie's haiku popped into her head. "Emily Grace brought us haiku written by the American girl who loved her. I would like to share one of the poems. It says,

'Emily Grace glows.
Her warm smile carries friendship.
Sunlight after rain.' "

Again, she saw smiles and approval. Headmaster Hanarai reached for the doll.

"I promised to keep her safe." The words burst from Chiyo, sounding as if she didn't trust the headmaster to take care of Emily Grace.

"You have done so," he assured her, taking the doll from her arms as if he did not hold a piece of her heart in his hands. "When we have finished here, you may spend an hour with your parents,

Miss Tamura. I understand they must leave for their home after that."

"*Arigatogozaimasu*, Headmaster Hanarai-san." She bowed, struggling against turning and running to her parents at once. They were going home so soon! She didn't want to lose one minute she could be spending with her family.

The headmaster beckoned to her and to all the girls who had returned from Tokyo, asking them to join the others on the platform in singing "The Welcome Song" to Emily Grace. Again torn two ways, Chiyo stood beside Hana and joined her voice to the others.

At last, the song ended. The headmaster spoke briefly, telling those gathered at the station how the Friendship Dolls had been sent to create peace between the two countries. "In two weeks, our school will hold a welcoming ceremony. Our girls are busy creating paper flowers to decorate a rickshaw. Emily Grace will be carried through town so that all may see and welcome her."

Chiyo glanced toward her parents, making sure they were still waiting. When could she go to them? She looked at Headmaster Hanarai, hoping to be dismissed, and saw Oki-sensei speaking to him. The teacher beamed at Chiyo.

Headmaster Hanarai exclaimed, "Miss Tamura, you have been honored! Oki-sensei has just told me you have been given a sketch of yourself done by master doll maker Hirata Gouyou."

"Yes, headmaster-san." Her voice sounded as uneasy as she felt.

"May I see it, Miss Tamura?"

She had already given up the doll! She had no choice but to bring out the drawing. She felt everyone staring at her as she reached into her pocket. "I mean to give it to my parents."

"Yes, of course." Headmaster unrolled the picture, studied it, then held it up for others to see. "The artist has captured your spirit, Miss Tamura. We at Tsuchiura Girls' School are as proud as your parents will be."

"*Arigatogozaimasu.*" She reached for the picture, but the headmaster had not finished.

He held it away, smiling as if doing her a favor. "Tsuchiura Girls' School will be happy to frame the drawing for you, if you will allow us to display it for a time."

Could she say no? What would happen if she said no? She wanted to snatch the drawing and run to *Okaasan* and *Otousan*. Headmaster Hanarai was already placing it in his briefcase, as if she had agreed. The question had not been a question. He meant to display the picture at the school whether she wanted him to or not.

She looked toward her parents and Yamada-san, hoping they would tell the headmaster to give back the drawing. Pride glowed from their faces.

For them, she would remain silent. She would be the humble girl they wished her to be. But the drawing was hers. It would never belong to the school.

At last, she was dismissed with the others. As people crowded around, she lost sight of the headmaster. She wove between people, needing to be with her parents. Others tried to speak to her, but she scarcely heard them and didn't stop moving.

When at last she reached her parents, proper manners flew from her head. Instead of a polite bow, she reached out to hug them both and felt their hands press warmly against her shoulders. Happy tears slipped down her cheeks. "I have missed you!"

"As we have missed you," her mother assured her.

Yamada Nori urged them all into his carriage to ride to a teahouse where they could visit before her parents had to return home. As the beautiful horse pulled them through the streets, questions swarmed through Chiyo. She struggled to keep them inside. Her family and Yamada-san had sent her away to school to learn humility, not to rain questions on them.

Even though she smiled and bowed and tried hard to act like a traditional girl, her mind raced while she toyed with her teacup. *Did you see the drawing?* she wanted to ask. *It's for you, to hang in the alcove. How are Yumi and Kimi? Is Masako preparing her three wedding kimonos? How I wish I could see them.*

"Yumi and her sister miss you," *Okaasan* murmured while the men talked together.

"I have so much to tell them!"

Yamada Nori must have seen anguish in her face. Gently, he said, "You will have much to share with your friends and family when you return, little sister. But let us talk of Tokyo and your discoveries there. Did you enjoy the ceremony?"

She thought of holding the forbidden doll, of being sent aside and told not to sing, of singing anyway, of the photographer . . . of her picture in the newspaper. Had they seen her picture?

None of those subjects were safe, and she reached almost blindly for one that would be acceptable.

"Miss Tokugawa accepted the first doll after welcoming the dolls to Japan. She was very graceful."

"You were wise to notice her graceful manners," Yamada-san said. "Have you become friends with Miss Miyamoto?"

Although he usually kept expression from his face, she could see the answer he expected in his eyes. He did not want to hear of the burned *kokeshi* or of Emily Grace stuffed into a vase.

What could she say? "Miss Miyamoto . . . is much like her father."

Yamada-san nodded. "The general is known to be forthright and well respected."

"He wants to destroy the dolls!" The words burst from her, and she dropped her chopsticks in dismay. Everyone stared at her.

"You misunderstood," *Otousan* said.

Chiyo felt her face flaming. Why had she thought General Miyamoto would be a safe subject? "He came to breakfast with us on the first morning. He said that welcoming the Friendship Dolls looked like weakness when our country should be expanding into others."

Okaasan sent warnings with her eyes, but it was too late to take the words back. Chiyo was afraid to look at Yamada-san.

"Ah, well," he said after a moment. "I have said he is forthright. Our emperor has welcomed the dolls. Therefore, all of Japan welcomes them."

Okaasan looked at her husband but spoke without his approving nod. Softly, she asked, "Chiyo-chan, is this girl difficult?"

Chiyo almost laughed at the question. Was Hoshi difficult? But *Otousan* and Yamada-san were watching her. "I understand Miss Miyamoto," she said, wanting to reassure her mother. "I think she understands me."

She glanced at Yamada Nori. "Her walk is very graceful, and she always speaks pleasantly. Only once have I heard her raise her voice, and that was in warning."

Otousan asked, "In warning? Of what, Chiyo-chan?"

She had plunged straight into the subject she wanted to avoid. "A doll fell. Hoshi called a warning, but I was closer. I caught the doll. It was Emily Grace." She looked uneasily at her mother. "A photographer took my picture."

"The one in the newspaper," Yamada-san said. "We have wondered how the photo came to be."

Otousan said, "Yamada-san brought a copy

of the newspaper to us. The picture is very good of you."

Okaasan added, "We framed it for the alcove, Chiyo-chan. When we look at the picture, we feel you near us."

Tears of relief swept through Chiyo, but she kept them from spilling. She had worried even more than she knew that the picture might change everything. Now, it seemed nothing had changed at all, and she could enjoy sharing the rest of her adventure. "The mayor sent an automobile for me! It was so big! And fast! When we drove down the street, boys ran after us shouting my name. Watanabe-sensei said I was a celebrity."

Her parents looked at each other. Had she said too much? She heard doubt in her voice as she asked softly, "Is a celebrity not a good thing to be?"

Okaasan patted her hand. "It is in the past. You have nothing to worry about but listening well to your teachers."

Otousan added quietly, "Chiyo-chan, we are honored to be your parents. It pleases us that you are learning so much."

In both of them, Chiyo saw the look that had been in her mother's eyes the day she warned that

Japan was changing and that Chiyo must go to the new school and learn to change with it.

All too soon, it was time for her to return there and for her parents and Yamada Nori to start for home. Chiyo bowed to her parents and especially to Yamada-san, who would be her brother when he married Masako.

"You made everything possible," she told him softly, wondering if she should have remained silent and simply bowed. "*Arigatogozaimasu.*"

Yamada-san nodded but looked at her with an unsmiling expression. "We did not expect such excitement for you when we sent you to this school. It is good that you are back in Tsuchiura now, where you will resume your training."

Chiyo considered the warning behind his words as she watched him help her parents into the carriage. He was not pleased with her picture after all. She must be careful never to attract attention to herself again.

For long moments, she lingered outside the school, watching the carriage roll away. She longed to be inside it, to be going home. In her memory, everyone at home was happy. Even Yumi only teased her because she loved her. Everyone there loved her. Her eyes blurred so that she had to keep blinking to hold the carriage in sight for as long as possible.

Behind her, the school door slid open. "Chiyo!" Hana shouted, rushing through. "Chiyo! You're back! I've been watching for you! Something awful has happened!"

CHAPTER 31

Emily Grace?" Disasters crowded into Chiyo's mind, each more terrible than the last. "Tell me! What's happened? Where is she?"

She grabbed for the door and pushed it wrong, jamming it.

Hana put one hand on the door. "She's fine. It's us!"

"Us?"

"The ones who went to Tokyo. We're doomed!"

"The ones who went to Tokyo?" Chiyo drew a deep breath, trying to think. "What do you mean? Headmaster is proud of us."

"He's too proud!" Hana moaned. "Kaito-sensei told us over tea to welcome us back. We are all to report on our trip. In front of the whole school! And parents! We have to talk in front of parents! I'm going to die!"

"I thought something awful had happened," Chiyo exclaimed.

"It has! Didn't you hear me? We have to give reports in front of the whole school. And parents! All of us!"

Fear for Emily Grace had kept Hana's words from sinking in. Talk in front of the whole school? In front of parents? "Oh." Chiyo heard her own voice sounding faint. "I thought we were supposed to be learning modesty."

"Kaito-sensei said modern girls will have to learn to talk when it's necessary. She said we may even work in business offices someday. Like those flappers in Tokyo, remember?"

Horrified, Chiyo asked, "She wants us to be flappers?"

"No." Hana giggled, then grew serious. "She said it will be good experience for us to tell everyone about our trip. And you . . ." She paused meaningfully. "You have the most to tell."

Chiyo swallowed. Hana was a politician's daughter. She should talk as easily as her father. *But I have never talked to a crowd, except to introduce Emily Grace at the station.* "When? Not today!"

"In two weeks. We're supposed to think about the trip and decide what we will tell everyone." Hana moaned again. "My mind is blank!"

Chiyo's mind didn't feel blank. It felt like a pot with too much rice boiling higher and spilling over. What should she tell them? How much? How little?

She tried to plan during the days following, days filled with classes and, in spare time, making paper flowers to decorate a rickshaw for the Friendship Doll's welcoming parade.

Emily Grace now sat on a small table in Headmaster's office. Every chance she got, Chiyo peeked through the door to make sure the doll was safe.

On the day they fastened the last of the paper flowers to the rickshaw, sunlight sparkled over the bright petals. Hana wore a large red blossom in her hair while she put the others into place.

Chiyo teased, "When I see that bright red flower, I almost forget I have to talk in front of many people."

"Maybe I should wear two flowers," Hana said. "One for me and one for you. We could both forget!"

The finished rickshaw was taken by night to the station and kept inside so townspeople would not see it before the parade.

When Chiyo removed the new kimono from its package in the morning, Hana helped her tie the obi and the *obi-jime.* The kimono fit as if she had been measured for it.

"It will give you courage for your report," Hana said, approving.

All the students gathered at the station to officially welcome Emily Grace, most of them wearing kimonos. Even more people than before gathered to see the doll from America. Headmaster Hanarai made a short speech about the friendship project. When he finished, Chiyo carried Emily Grace from inside the station, feeling almost as graceful as Hoshi.

It felt right to hold the doll in her arms again and to sing "The Welcome Song" with the others. She gazed at Emily Grace when she reached the line *"This, our land of flowers, is now your own."*

She was sure that the doll's eyes held a warm glow. It was even harder to present her to

Headmaster Hanarai once again. Headmaster held the doll high for people to admire, even those in the back of the crowd, before carrying her to the flower-covered rickshaw. People bowed deeply. Their sparkling eyes said even more.

The girls who had gone to Tokyo were to pull the rickshaw through town. Hoshi announced that she would walk in front, since she was the leader. No one questioned her, although Chiyo thought that Hoshi should walk with the others and help pull.

Headmaster Hanarai settled Emily Grace on a cushion in the center of the rickshaw seat.

"She's too small to see," Chiyo exclaimed. "All they'll see is flowers!"

"We'll fix that." He lifted Chiyo onto the seat. "Hold her up so everyone can see."

Startled, Chiyo sat in the center of the flower-strewn seat and held Emily Grace in her lap. A look from Hoshi made her glad she was riding. If she were pulling one of the handles, Hoshi would probably trip her in front of the moving wheels.

The pleasure on people's faces made her even happier. She held up the doll, smiling and waving Emily Grace's arm. No one seemed to notice Hoshi gliding ahead of the cart, nodding royally while the people bowed and smiled at Chiyo and Emily Grace.

Many followed the rickshaw to the school, crowding into the largest room, the one used for dance classes, to see Emily Grace again and to ask questions. Almost before Chiyo knew it was time, she found herself sitting in the front row with the five other girls. The two teachers who had shared the trip with them sat at one side.

Chiyo felt like Hana, as if her mind had suddenly become blank. She had planned for days, but now she had no idea what to say.

CHAPTER 32

Hoshi spoke first. Her father was present, glancing at his watch before the reports began. Chiyo thought he looked as if he didn't want to be there, couldn't wait to leave, and had probably come only to criticize whatever he heard, but Hoshi's eyes shone. It was her chance to impress him.

Again, Chiyo felt reluctant sympathy. Her own father would be as near the front as possible, trying to look well mannered while wanting to break into a big smile.

"Tokyo is a busy, exciting city," Hoshi began. "It can frighten country girls more accustomed to chasing goats than riding in rickshaws and automobiles."

She glanced toward Chiyo and Hana with a faint smile. "Since I was no stranger to the city, I saw a chance for leadership. I led the other girls whenever I could."

Chiyo began to regret her earlier sympathy. She whispered to Hana beside her, "What would we have done without her?"

Hana's eyes sparkled. "We were helpless."

Hoshi ignored them. "I helped the girls select a rickshaw and explained sights we passed, such as the shrines." She smiled at Headmaster Hanarai. "I would like to thank Tsuchiura Girls' School for the opportunity to grow as a leader."

Hana nudged Chiyo and they both hid smiles.

Tomi spoke next, describing silk kimonos in Tokyo shop windows that were as pretty as the wings of butterflies. Shizuko spoke of the big welcoming ceremony with classes of American girls from the Tokyo school. "We all sang together," she said, "except for Chiyo."

Chiyo realized that this was not the first time Shizuko had made her look bad. *Shizuko wants to be like the worst parts of Hoshi.*

Shizuko's cheeks reddened as if she had

embarrassed herself with the comment. "But Chiyo got to be in the newspaper and on a poster," she added quickly. "We're all proud of her."

Chiyo twisted her fingers together in her lap, remembering that those things had happened because she broke her promise to avoid touching any of the dolls from America. Would someone mention that? She wished the reports were over.

Kimiko also talked of the welcoming ceremony and of the exchange of dolls between the American ambassador's daughter and Miss Tokugawa Yukiko. "Miss Tokugawa is the granddaughter of the great shogun. We were honored to share the ceremony with her."

Hana spoke then, telling of a Westerner in the hotel who wore a casual kimono with the lapels crossed from the wrong side, the way they would be arranged if he were dead. "Whenever we saw him in the hotel, we asked each other behind our hands, 'Shall we bow to the dead man?'"

Several students laughed, and parents smiled. The teachers were less amused. Oki-sensei said sternly, "Miss Nakata, surely you saw something more impressive in Tokyo than a man wearing his kimono in the wrong way."

"*Hai*," Hana said quickly. "We met master doll

maker Hirata Gouyou and saw the beautiful dolls he makes. He let us each choose a *kokeshi* to take home. Here is mine." She drew the little doll from a fold of her kimono and held it up for everyone to see.

Chiyo listened to the others with a sinking feeling. They had talked of so many things. What else was there for her to say? Oki-sensei called her name, and she walked to the front of the room and bowed to the class and to the parents. She was tempted to say that they hadn't needed Hoshi to tell them which rickshaw to choose, but remembered Hoshi's father. She would not embarrass Hoshi in front of him.

"Tokyo is big and very interesting," she said. "The mayor of Tokyo sent his automobile to bring me to his office. It smelled nice inside."

Watanabe-sensei asked, "And why did the mayor send his personal automobile, Miss Tamura?"

"He wanted to have his picture taken with me." Her face heated. It felt like bragging to say such a thing, but it was true. "Watanabe-sensei went with me to help me know the right things to say. I had never met a mayor before."

People chuckled, sounding sympathetic. Watanabe-sensei said gently, "Everyone will enjoy hearing what the mayor gave you."

"The mayor gave me this medal." She was wearing it on a ribbon over her new kimono and held it out so everyone could see. "It says I am to protect Emily Grace and keep her safe. And I did. I carried her all the way from Tokyo and showed her the view from the window of the train."

Headmaster Hanarai took Watanabe-sensei's place as speaker. "Miss Tamura is a modest young lady, as are all our students. She has not mentioned another gift given her in Tokyo." He held up the drawing, now in a black lacquer frame. "Hirata Gouyou-san, who has become a master doll maker while still a young man, presented Miss Tamura with a drawing of herself. Hers is to be the face of a doll he is creating to be sent to America."

Chiyo grew warm with embarrassment. Everyone looking at her made her uneasy. She noticed several murmuring together. She hoped they were not saying that the hill village girl did not deserve such honor and that Miyamoto Hoshi should have been chosen.

She waited for Headmaster to give her the picture, but he was saying that it would be displayed next to the door into his office. Anyone who liked might see it there.

But it's mine! she objected in silence. *It's for my parents.*

Headmaster ended the meeting by inviting guests to talk with the girls who had made the trip. To Chiyo's surprise, General Miyamoto approached her. "I find it interesting that Hirata Gouyou should select you as a model, Miss Tamura."

Embarrassment flushed through Chiyo. It was hard enough to find the courage to speak to Hoshi's father. How could she answer him? She was afraid to risk a glance at his face and tried to understand his tone. Did he believe she was immodest to have posed for the artist?

But his voice had been warm and even sounded friendly when he added, "You used your time well in Tokyo, Miss Tamura. You are to be congratulated."

"*Arigatogozaimasu,*" she murmured. When she raised her head from a respectful bow, her gaze met Hoshi's. The girl stood behind her father, looking furious that Chiyo had received the rare praise that should have been hers.

"I have tried to be like Hoshi," Chiyo said. It

wasn't exactly true, but she hoped that General Miyamoto would compliment his daughter, too.

"You were yourself," he said. "It was enough."

Behind him, Hoshi's eyes narrowed, her brows lost their arch, and her mouth turned down in a dangerously stormy expression.

CHAPTER 33

Hoshi's stormy glare stayed with Chiyo through the rest of the day and into the next morning. That expression had been like a boulder poised above the village. The slightest push might send it tumbling down the canyon, causing damage all the way.

Chiyo started for Headmaster's office to peek in at Emily Grace but saw the doll on a carved stand in a recess outside the door with the drawing displayed nearby. She stopped, looking from one to the other while fear fought with longing. Hana approached, looking worried. "Are you afraid Hoshi is going to do something awful? You can't watch all the time."

That was exactly what she needed to do. Plans flew through Chiyo's head. "I only need to watch between classes and during lunch."

"You might be late to class."

"No, I won't. Hoshi is never late. As soon as I see her go into the classroom, I'll go in, too."

"Hoshi's quick. What if you see her brush ink over the doll or slash her with a knife? What will you do?"

"I'll jump in front of Emily Grace to save her." And she would, too, if that moment actually came.

Her plan worked for two days. On the third afternoon, Kaito-sensei stepped in front of her. "Miss Tamura, it does not look well for you to pose with your picture during every class break. Students are talking about you. A humble Japanese girl never causes talk."

Pose! Chiyo struggled to swallow the sting of the accusation. "I'm not posing, Sensei. I'm guarding. I'm afraid something will happen to our doll."

Sensei looked even more offended. "What harm could come to the doll here in our school? You must learn trust, Miss Tamura, along with humility."

"But Sensei—"

The teacher cut off Chiyo's attempt to explain.

"I was sorry to see you join the group going to Tokyo. You were not ready for such a trip, and you were certainly not ready for all that happened there."

Did Kaito-sensei believe that? The unfairness cut through Chiyo, and she couldn't help protesting, "Even General Miyamoto said—"

Again, the teacher stopped her. "You have a great deal to learn yet about humility. I do not want to see you posing here again. Vanity is not attractive."

Chiyo felt the words burn. She had taken Hoshi's sarcasm and kept silent. Scolding from her teacher was too much. She knew she wasn't vain. It wasn't fair for Sensei to say so.

"I didn't want to be in the newspapers!" The words burst from her. "Or on a poster! Or on a doll! I just want to be an ordinary girl!"

She realized that Hoshi had come from a classroom in the midst of the outburst. Hoshi was seeing her revenge without doing a thing. That knowledge lodged pain deeper in Chiyo's throat than the teacher's words.

Sensei's mouth set in a severe line. "I had not thought you to be excitable, Miss Tamura. Clearly, becoming a minor celebrity has been damaging to you."

Chiyo stared at the floor. *Celebrity.* That was another thing she had not wanted.

"You are excused from the remaining afternoon classes," the teacher said. "You are to rest in your room. I advise you to think of the sacrifices your family made to send you here."

Yamada Nori-san sent me here. He believes in me. So do my parents. She had already said too much and would only get herself into deeper trouble if she said more. She bowed respectfully and, sick inside, walked across the courtyard toward the stairs.

She had tried to fit in and what did it get her? *A lecture she didn't deserve!*

It's not fair! The words swirling in her head gradually faded. By the time she pulled her futon from the closet, her mother's face came into her mind. She saw again the unexpected fire in *Okaasan*'s eyes and in her voice as she said Chiyo must go to Tsuchiura. *"Put fear behind and seize this opportunity."*

Chiyo felt as if *Okaasan* said those words again now. Somehow, they meant even more than they had at the time. Her parents expected her to learn from Tsuchiura Girls' School. They were pleased she had been to Tokyo and had met the mayor and the doll maker.

They trust me, she thought. *Why doesn't Sensei trust me?* She spread the futon, picturing home, but as she lay on the mat, she made a silent promise. She would not go home until she had made her parents and Yamada-san proud.

She must convince Kaito-sensei that she was still a modest traditional girl, the girl her parents wanted her to be, the girl the school wanted her to be. *I'll tell her right now,* Chiyo decided. *I will bow so low my forehead will touch the floor. And I'll apologize. Then everything will be right.*

By letting anger show, she had only pleased Hoshi.

She went quietly down the stairs and across the courtyard, but at the closed doorway, she realized that class was still in session. Sensei would not wish to be interrupted, and as much as Chiyo wanted to apologize, she did not intend to bow to the floor in front of all the girls.

She would have to wait until after school. As she turned to the stairs, doors opened and girls rushed from some rooms and into others, hurrying to music or dance, mathematics or calligraphy. All of them talked and laughed as if this day were no different from any other day.

For them, it wasn't different. For Chiyo, it felt like the worst day of her life. She returned to the second building, climbed the stairs, and lay again on her sleeping mat. Sometime later, she woke with a start. She hadn't dreamed it. Hana was shouting her name from the doorway.

"What is it?" Chiyo sat up, rubbing her eyes. Hana's expression made no sense. She looked scared and angry at the same time. Something had happened. Something bad.

"Headmaster wants to see you. In his office. Right now!"

"Why?"

But Hana was already running down the stairs. Chiyo scrambled to her feet, smoothing her clothes and hair as she rushed after Hana.

All along the walkway, students fell silent, then moved back to leave a clear path to the headmaster's office. Chiyo wanted to ask what had happened, but as her stomach twisted, she wasn't sure she wanted to know.

When she stepped into the office, the room wavered like a reflection in water when a stone has disturbed the surface. Only Headmaster Hanarai's desk remained clear and, on top of it, what was left of Emily Grace.

The sleeves and ruffles of the doll's dress were ripped half off. Her arms and legs were missing. Bits of broken rubber bands showed through the empty sockets of her hollow body. Someone had cut Emily Grace into pieces.

CHAPTER 34

"Noooo!" It took long moments before Chiyo realized that the scream was hers. She wanted to throw herself at Emily Grace, to protect her. But it was too late.

Headmaster Hanarai sat behind the desk. Kaito-sensei stood at one side. Chiyo had never seen them look so grim. Those expressions kept her frozen in the doorway instead of rushing to the doll. Her scream echoed around her.

"We would like you to tell us what happened," the headmaster said.

Somehow, Chiyo managed to remain standing on wobbly legs while anger poured through her entire body. Sensei had made her leave her doll unprotected. And this had happened.

Accusation in their eyes made the headmaster's meaning suddenly clear through the horror: *We would like you to tell us what happened.*

She turned toward him as if she couldn't turn her eyes without turning her body. "You think I did that? I would never . . . I love Emily Grace."

She stepped forward to reach out almost blindly and lift the limbless body. The doll's lashes swept up. "Mama."

Chiyo's hands trembled so hard the rubber bands inside Emily Grace slapped back and forth. Shaking, she cradled the doll. "I would never hurt her. Never!"

Emily Grace had become far more than a doll. She had become almost real. Now she was hurt. She was crying for help. And no help was coming.

"We found the arms and legs," Kaito-sensei said in a voice so deeply disappointed it carried more sorrow than anger. "They were hidden within your desk where you left them. The knife was there as well."

The arms and legs weren't destroyed. Relief rushed in, then vanished. They were accusing her with that information. "I didn't hurt her! I wouldn't!"

"Miss Tamura," Headmaster Hanarai warned, "do not add lies to dishonor. You were seen hiding the doll parts in your desk."

"How could someone see me do something I didn't do? Something I would never do?"

Hoshi! She knew suddenly. Hoshi hated her for many things, but especially for the praise from General Miyamoto. Chiyo almost said so, but Hoshi's father was important to the school. They would take Hoshi's word over hers. She could only say again, "It wasn't me."

"Miss Tamura," the headmaster said, "two witnesses have come forward, one who saw you with the doll parts, another who saw you on the stairs between classes."

Hope for the truth slipped further from her reach.

Kaito-sensei added, "You were sent to your sleeping area, but you did not stay there. Did you, Miss Tamura?"

"I . . . came down. I wanted to talk to you, Sensei, to apologize." Chiyo's throat tightened. She couldn't get the rest of it out. *I wanted to tell you I'm still a humble traditional girl.*

Headmaster's brows came together. "It saddens me to learn that Kaito-sensei was right in saying you should not go to Tokyo. It was only by chance you took Fujii Michi's place. Watanabe-sensei did not check with me before adding you to the group."

The damage to Emily Grace made Chiyo feel so sick, she could hardly hear the awful things Headmaster was saying.

His sharp tone forced her to listen. "Clearly you were not ready for so much attention. Kaito-sensei has told me of your unbecoming outburst. You remained angry and returned while the others were in class to do this terrible thing. I believe you meant to be caught, Miss Tamura. You meant to be sent home."

"I protected her," Chiyo said, her voice barely above a whisper. She felt stunned that they would say such things to her, that they would believe such things of her. "I promised the mayor. I kept her safe all the way from Tokyo."

"Once the damage was done," the headmaster continued, ignoring her protest, "you realized what it would mean to be sent home in shame. You hid the doll parts while classes were changing and sneaked back upstairs."

"No!"

Again, Headmaster ignored her. "This doll is no longer fit for anything but the trash heap. You have your wish, Miss Tamura. We have sent word to Yamada Nori to remove you from our school."

He might as well have added, *where hill country girls like you do not belong*. He had not wanted her here in the first place. What would happen now? Would Yamada Nori enroll her in still another distant school? In her mind, the imaginary scale of good conduct collapsed and with it, her dream of going home for Masako's wedding. She could only say again, "I didn't hurt her. *I wouldn't*."

"Return to your room," Headmaster said in a voice that didn't allow for argument. "You will leave tomorrow. I do not expect to see you again."

Chiyo opened her mouth to protest. She closed it. She couldn't hammer with words against a wall as stony as the one she saw in the headmaster's face.

Someone knows the truth, she told herself to keep tears at bay. *Someone must know. I have to find out who it is. I have to make them tell Headmaster what really happened*.

She started for the door but couldn't help looking back a last time at what was left of Emily Grace.

The headmaster had turned to his assistant. "Send for the janitor. Have this cleared away."

"*No!*" Chiyo cried out. "Don't throw her in the trash! Please!"

Headmaster's voice held solid ice. "You are dismissed."

"But . . ." The doll's eyes were closed again. "She needs help. She can be fixed. I'm sure she can!"

"Out!"

The headmaster's roar sent Chiyo stumbling from the office. Curious students at every side called out, "What happened? Is it the doll? Did you cut her?"

Chiyo ran past them and all the way to the silence of her sleeping mat. She flung herself onto the futon.

One thought ran again and again through her head. *Someone knows the truth. Someone will tell.* "But I'll be far away by then," she said aloud. "Even if they apologize, I'm *never* coming back!"

She didn't know where she would go. Maybe Yamada Nori would take her to still another school, but her hope for Masako's wedding was gone. "Masako will understand," she whispered, as if Emily Grace could hear her.

Headmaster meant to throw Emily Grace in the trash! *Her body isn't broken. Her face isn't smashed. Whoever hurt her didn't ruin her.*

"You can be fixed, Emily Grace," Chiyo said to the distant doll. Fixing her was more important than proving who had hurt her. "Hirata Gouyou could fix you." He would, too, if he could see her.

She sat up straight. Maybe he *could* see her.

Slowly, a plan took shape. Trash was collected while people were still sleeping, but she was a country girl. She was used to getting up before dawn. And there was something else. While up before sunrise doing chores for the school, she often heard the early train leaving the station on its way to Tokyo.

Did she dare make the trip alone? Headmaster had said her promise ended when she brought the doll safely to Tsuchiura. In her heart, the promise had not ended. She loved Emily Grace. She must do all she could to have the doll repaired. And when she came back with the doll looking new again, Headmaster would have to give her a good report. Wouldn't he?

There was hope. Hope for Emily Grace. And

maybe, if everything went right, hope for Masako's wedding.

Chiyo pulled out her small purse with the coins from the Tokyo mayor, two gold coins she had never mentioned to anyone, along with a single sen. Was it enough to pay her fare? It would have to be.

She looked around her mat. What else should she take? Her sewing kit. She would need to repair the doll's dress. She hesitated, then slipped out of her school uniform and put on the new kimono. She would not leave that behind.

She couldn't tie the obi properly at her back but did the best she could. Footsteps sounded on the stairs. The other girls were coming. Quickly, she slipped onto her futon and pulled the blanket to her chin to hide the kimono.

Hana was first through the door, rushing to her. "Are you all right?"

"No," Chiyo said. "They want to throw Emily Grace out like trash."

"They haven't yet," Tomi said from her mat farther down.

"They've put the pieces on the carved stand outside Headmaster's office," Hana explained. "She's serving as a lesson to us to control our tempers."

With sarcasm, Tomi said, "A proper Japanese girl does not let emotion control her. That's what Kaito-sensei told us."

Shizuko unrolled her futon without looking at Chiyo. She usually offered at least a shy smile. Her silence was accusation.

"I didn't do that to the doll," Chiyo said. Shizuko pretended not to hear.

"And I don't care what you think," Chiyo added, to hide the hurt that Shizuko would suspect the worst of her. In the hotel, she had been as quick as Hoshi to think the doll was stolen.

"Of course you didn't hurt Emily Grace," Hana exclaimed. "You love her."

Tomi added, "Everybody knows that!"

"Do they?" Shizuko asked softly, as she pulled her blanket to her chin.

"Don't mind her," Tomi said. "She's become friends with Hoshi. I saw Hoshi share a sweet with her."

"Never mind," Chiyo said. "None of this matters. The school has called Yamada-san to remove me from Tsuchiura Girls' School."

"No!" Hana protested, while Tomi pressed one hand over her mouth.

Only to herself Chiyo added, *But I won't be here. I'm glad to know Emily Grace is on the stand. I won't have to dig through the trash in my new kimono to find her. While everyone else is sleeping, Emily Grace and I will be on our way to Tokyo and Hirata Gouyou.*

CHAPTER 35

Near dawn, Chiyo slipped from her mat and smoothed her kimono. The others would wake soon to do their chores. For now, all she heard was their steady breathing and wind whispering through tree branches.

Moonlight made it easy to see Emily Grace lying in pieces on the carved stand, just as Hana had said. Chiyo swallowed a sob. "Don't worry, Emily Grace," she whispered. "I'm going to take care of you, the way I promised I would."

Yamada Nori would come to the school today expecting to take her away. If he had to wait for her to come back from Tokyo, he might want nothing more to do with her.

She's my responsibility, she told him silently. *I have to save her.*

Gently, she lifted the doll's head and body onto a square of cloth. She added the arms and legs, then pulled the corners together and tied them.

She turned to Hirata Gouyou's sketch. It belonged to her, not to the school. As she reached for the frame to take the picture out, she heard footsteps.

There was no time. With an anguished glance toward her picture, she clutched the bundle with Emily Grace. As silently as possible, keeping to shadows, she hurried from the school.

It was farther to the station than she remembered from the rickshaw ride. With nearly every step, she glanced back, afraid someone from the school was running after her.

Would anyone have noticed that the doll was missing? No. The students would think the janitor had thrown her away. The teachers and headmaster might think that, too. Maybe no one had even looked on the carved stand. They wouldn't *want* to remember poor cut-up Emily Grace.

"They won't miss me, either," she told the doll. "They'll think I'm upstairs waiting for my ride."

She listened for the train whistle, afraid she

would miss it. At last she saw the station ahead. Rushing inside, she put her two precious ten-yen coins on the counter. "I need a ticket to Tokyo, please."

The station agent glanced at the coins. "A ticket is twenty-five yen. That's not enough."

She looked into her purse as if expecting to find another gold coin, but all it held was the single sen. She would need a hundred sen to make even one more yen.

"That's all I have!" She leaned over the counter, closer to the agent. "I have to go to Tokyo on the next train. It's important!"

"Not enough," he said again.

Far down the tracks, the train whistled. The sound cut through her. She pushed the coins toward the agent. "Where will this much take me?"

He became interested enough to be suspicious. "I thought you had to go to Tokyo."

"I do! But I know somebody in . . ." She thought fast and remembered a town on the Tone River, the one where Emily Grace had waved to people celebrating a local festival. ". . . in Toride. A friend. She'll take me the rest of the way. Do I have enough to go to Toride?"

The agent picked up the coins. The floorboards

vibrated as the train roared into the station. How long would it wait? Chiyo shifted from one foot to the other while the agent slowly put the coins into a drawer.

She wanted to ask him to hurry but didn't dare. He might decide that she shouldn't have a ticket at all. How long had she been away from the school? *Was* somebody looking?

At last, the agent handed her a ticket marked Toride, Ibaraki Prefecture. She shoved it into her purse with her single remaining sen and ran to the platform.

The conductor was just swinging onto the train. "Wait!" Chiyo called, snatching out her ticket. "I'm coming with you!" Hugging the bundle with Emily Grace, she ran across the platform.

The conductor reached out to lift her into a passenger car. She walked toward an empty seat, jolting off balance as the train rolled ahead, but never letting go of Emily Grace. After all but falling into an empty pair of seats, she scooted to the window for a last view of Tsuchiura.

"Don't worry, Emily Grace," she said softly. "At Toride, farmers will be taking produce to the Tokyo markets. We'll ride the rest of the way on a wagon."

She thought of letting Emily Grace watch the passing houses and trees with her, but it might look strange to the few other passengers if she held an armless and legless doll to the window. They would remember her, if anyone asked. After a few minutes, she leaned back in the seat and closed her eyes.

It seemed only minutes before the conductor called her awake. "We're coming into Toride, miss. You don't want to pass your stop."

It was nice of him to warn her, she told herself. She'd have been glad of it if she *wanted* to go to Toride. Or if she really knew someone there who would take her to Tokyo.

When she walked from the station, her heart sank. The sun had risen while she slept. Farmers going to Tokyo left before dawn to be at the markets by sunrise.

The road was empty now, except for an occasional automobile, and those all zipped past. Farther along, hope rose when she saw an approaching truck with caged chickens in the back. It passed on by as if the driver were used to seeing a girl in a kimono standing beside the road.

Another car passed her, then later, a carriage moving fast behind two horses, both heading toward Tokyo. Neither slowed. The sky looked heavy with the kind of rain that would fall steadily all day. A first drop spattered her new kimono. She rubbed it with her hand, trying to dry the silk.

"We might be in trouble, Emily Grace," she said softly. Another drop spattered the kimono. Again she wiped it away, this time choking back a sob.

A car rumbled up the road behind her. As she looked around, a raindrop hit her face. She blinked, then blinked again, thinking she must be seeing things. Was the car really slowing? It was stopping!

A young woman with short hair swinging across her cheekbones leaned from a window. A pretty headband circled her forehead. "Hey, kiddo!" she called. "Need help?"

Where was the driver? Could a car drive itself? That wouldn't be any stranger than for a woman, even a flapper, to be driving it.

Chiyo wanted to answer *hai*, she needed a ride, but she wasn't at all sure she wanted one with a flapper behind the wheel.

CHAPTER 36

The woman left the car and came around to sit on her heels in front of Chiyo. *Okaasan* would have been shocked by the fringed blue dress that barely covered her knees. "What's happened, kiddo? Why are you out here alone in your pretty kimono? You're coming all apart!"

She turned Chiyo around and with quick fingers tied the obi properly.

Chiyo looked over her shoulder. "Are you a flapper?"

The woman grinned. "You got it, kiddo. But what about you? Do your parents know you're out here? It's going to rain hard in a few minutes. You'd better run home."

"I don't live here." Chiyo gulped as everything hit her at once. Words tumbled out as if that rock balanced above her village had come loose, shaking a rush of words from her.

"My school blamed me for something awful, but I didn't do it. I wouldn't," she explained. "They were going to send me away, so I left. But I only had money enough to ride the train to Toride."

The flapper sat back on her heels. "What kind of awful thing could they blame on a sweet girl like you?"

Chiyo opened the cloth a little to show the doll. "This is Emily Grace. She came all the way from America to my school. I promised to take care of her, but someone cut her into pieces. Headmaster was going to throw her in the trash! So I'm taking her to Tokyo."

The flapper folded the cloth back a little more. When she saw the loose arms and legs and the cut pieces of rubber bands in the empty sockets, she drew in a soft breath. "Someone didn't like this pretty doll."

Chiyo's eyes blurred. *It's the rain*, she told herself fiercely, and wrapped the cloth over Emily

Grace. "She didn't hurt anybody and now she's all in pieces! I have to get her to a doll maker I know."

The flapper put one hand gently on Chiyo's shoulder. "The school must be looking for you."

"No. They just want city girls in their school. I'm from a village in the mountains. They didn't want me in the first place. Now they want to forget me."

The woman looked into her eyes. "You may be judging them a little harshly, but I can see why you're upset. You're sure this doll maker will repair her?"

"*Hai!*" There was no doubt in Chiyo's mind. She drew a deep breath, going against all she had been taught, to ask a stranger for a ride. "Please, will you take me closer to Tokyo?"

The woman looked around, as if hoping one of Chiyo's teachers would appear. "Someone must be looking for you."

"No." Chiyo knew that her face looked as sad as she felt inside. "Please take me as far as you're going. I can walk the rest of the way. I'm used to walking."

There were no pedestrians in sight. An occasional automobile went past without stopping. Decision settled in the woman's face. "I'm a nurse at the hospital in Tokyo. I don't think my doctors can fix your doll, but I can take you to the doll maker."

Joy leaped through Chiyo. She scarcely noticed the raindrops. She couldn't help asking, "A nurse? Aren't nurses men? Like doctors?"

The woman's smile made her eyes sparkle. "You'll see more of us, kiddo. A few years ago, only thirteen thousand women worked as nurses in all of Japan. Now I'm one of more than fifty-seven thousand."

Chiyo thought of the flappers in the restaurant who all worked in a business office. *Okaasan* was right. Japan was changing. "Do you have to be a flapper to be a nurse?"

Laughter burst from the woman. "No, but if you are a nurse or in any job where you have made your own choice, you can choose to be a flapper . . . or to do anything else you like."

Even to drive a car. Chiyo had never seen a woman handle any kind of machinery unless she counted the rice huller at home.

"Your nice kimono is getting wet," the nurse warned. "You don't want to stand out here in the rain."

"No," Chiyo agreed. It took courage to climb into the motorcar, but she had to get Emily Grace to the doll maker even more than she needed to get her kimono out of the rain. She sat on the edge of the front seat while the flapper turned a crank, just as the mayor's driver had. When the motor caught, she hurried around to climb inside.

Chiyo clutched the seat so hard her knuckles turned white. This was not like riding behind the mayor's uniformed driver. The car didn't feel as solid, either. It rumbled noisily along, and she felt every bump under the tires.

"I'm Yaeko, by the way," the woman told her. "What's your name?"

"Tamura Chiyo." It was hard to talk when she was holding her breath and staring out the windshield. She couldn't help feeling as if they might run off the pavement if she looked away. But she was going to Tokyo!

The woman had introduced herself by her first name. What was Chiyo supposed to call her? It might be safer not to call her anything, but she couldn't help asking, "Does it cost a lot to buy your own automobile?"

She heard amusement in Yaeko's answer. "Yes.

This one belongs to a doctor at my hospital. To tell you a secret, he's sweet on me. He thought it was a lark to teach me to drive."

Chiyo nodded. Adults lived in a world different from hers, especially adults in Tokyo. She knew that *Otousan* would never teach *Okaasan* to drive, or loan her his car, if he had one. *Okaasan* would never agree if he did offer.

"Does the ride scare you, Chiyo-chan?"

Chiyo sat a little straighter. "I rode in a car before. With the mayor of Tokyo."

"Oh, yes? Traveling in high company, were you?" The sparkle was back in the nurse's eyes. Then Yaeko looked at her for so long that Chiyo wanted to urge her to watch the road. "Say," the nurse exclaimed, "you're the girl from the poster! Your face is all over Tokyo. And this is the doll!"

Chiyo nodded, pulling her gaze from the road to look down at Emily Grace bundled in her lap.

"Someone got jealous, huh?"

"The teachers think I hurt her! But it wasn't me! I would never hurt her! I love her!"

"Of course you do! If your teachers can't see that, they've had their noses in their books for too long."

Chiyo was surprised to feel a laugh bubble up

when she'd thought she would never laugh or even smile again. She looked out at the road flying by. Even the mayor's car hadn't gone this fast. Maybe it could, but had to go slow in the city. The speed amazed and thrilled her. "Maybe someday I will drive."

"I'm sure you will," Yaeko agreed. "I can tell you're a free spirit at heart."

Chiyo thought again of the women in the restaurant smoking cigarettes and looking boldly at men. "No," she said quickly. "No, I will go home to my village when my sister is married." She wished Masako's wedding was today. Or yesterday!

"Your sister?"

"She is marrying a man who wants me to be a traditional Japanese girl. I must know how to act when I visit Masako's new home. That's why I was going to school in Tsuchiura instead of my village. He thinks school will teach me to be serene."

"Is that working?"

Chiyo looked at Emily Grace. "Not yet." And now it never would. She swallowed hard and looked ahead.

She soon realized that Yaeko liked sound better than silence. The nurse had begun to sing a song about a red, red robin.

"What are you singing?" Chiyo asked when Yaeko paused.

The nurse glanced at her. "Ever hear of a guy called Al Jolson?"

Chiyo shook her head. What kind of name was that?

"No, I guess you wouldn't have. He's in vaudeville in America, and now he's acting and singing in moving pictures. That was his number one song last year." She glanced at Chiyo. "Would you like to learn the words?"

Chiyo almost said no, but why not? Kaito-sensei and the others weren't here to frown. "*Hai*," she said instead. "But they aren't in Japanese."

"Then you'll learn a little English." Yaeko taught her a line. As they sang it together, the scenery flew past. Chiyo's voice blended with the nurse's and brought an approving smile. They both laughed when she made mistakes.

Together, they sang about living, loving, and being happy. Yaeko grinned at her after translating the song into Japanese. "Those are words to live by, kiddo."

Chiyo felt far from her parents' goal of learning to behave like a modest Japanese girl, but she wasn't in the village now. And she liked singing with Yaeko, even words that were silly but sometimes made sense.

"This man your sister's marrying," Yaeko said after a while, "the one who expects school to change you? He's right, Chiyo-chan, but not in the way he thinks."

"What do you mean?"

"The world is your oyster, Tamura Chiyo. And I can tell you've got the nerve to swallow it whole."

"Even the pearl?"

The nurse laughed. "Especially the pearl, kiddo. Especially the pearl!"

Rain was falling harder when they reached Tokyo. Yaeko turned a handle back and forth to brush long thin wipers across the outside of the windshield. What a clever vehicle the automobile was. Chiyo couldn't imagine any way to make it better.

When she recognized the railroad station, she directed Yaeko from there to the old-on-one-side, new-on-the-other street where the doll maker lived.

Yaeko twisted the wheel abruptly to turn the car away from rails. "Oops. Here comes a streetcar."

Yaeko's little car rocked from side to side when

the streetcar rushed by. "How does it move?" Chiyo asked. "Horses aren't pulling it. And it doesn't have room for a big engine."

"Electricity, kiddo. See those wires overhead? We live in a modern age." The flapper drove across the rails and pulled to a stop in front of the dark house with a slanting roof that Chiyo remembered from her earlier visit.

The nurse leaned over the seat and lifted a bright yellow parasol from the back. "You take this with you. Try to keep your pretty kimono dry."

"But it's yours."

Yaeko smiled. "It's my gift to Emily Grace. We can't have her getting wet after all she's suffered."

"Arigatogozaimasu," Chiyo murmured, willing to accept the parasol for Emily Grace, if not for herself.

"Now listen, Chiyo-chan," Yaeko said, looking unusually serious as she leaned across to open the passenger door. "You said the doll maker knows people at your school, so he'll know what to do. But if things don't work out like you hope, you get someone to bring you to the hospital—St. Luke's. Remember that. When you get there, ask for me, okay?"

"*Hai*, but I'm sure he will help me." Chiyo climbed to the street, her attention shifting to the doll maker's house.

Yaeko called, "Chiyo?"

When Chiyo looked back, Yaeko grinned. "Live, love, and be happy, kiddo."

Chiyo grinned back at her, turning the bright yellow parasol over her head like a flower in the rain. "I promise!"

In her arms, the doll shifted. "Mama!" Chiyo's laughter vanished. Turning from the car, she ran across the flat gray stone to the door. Urgency drove her, and she knocked harder than she meant. From beyond the door, footsteps padded toward her.

CHAPTER 37

Part of Chiyo noticed that Yaeko did not drive away until the door opened and Mrs. Sasaki looked out, but the nurse was in the past now. Chiyo faced the doll maker's unsmiling gatekeeper demon of a housekeeper. She clutched the bundle tighter to hold Emily Grace inside. "Please, Mrs. Sasaki, I have to see Hirata-san. It's important."

Mrs. Sasaki's mouth pinched in a tight line. "Hirata-san has a guest. He cannot see you." She began to close the door.

Chiyo wedged one elbow between the door and the sill. "It's important! I have to see the doll maker!"

The housekeeper pressed the door against Chiyo's arm, but even she seemed unwilling to cause pain and did not press hard. "I cannot help you. You are not expected and you are not welcome."

"It's Emily Grace." Chiyo raised her voice, trying to call past the housekeeper. "The American doll. Someone hurt her. She needs the doll maker!"

The door pressed harder. Maybe the housekeeper didn't mind causing pain, after all.

Chiyo refused to pull her arm back. If that door shut, she would have nowhere to go. "Please, Mrs. Sasaki. Please, it's so important!"

The housekeeper glared. "I've told you, Hirata-san has a visitor. He has no time for you. Go!"

She pushed Chiyo's elbow from the door and closed it. Chiyo stumbled back, nearly dropping Emily Grace. She clutched the doll closer. "Hirata Gouyou-san will see us, Emily Grace. I know he will. We just have to let him know we're here."

She walked along the side of the house, trying to think where his workshop would be. Near the back, she heard men's voices through a partly open window. She hesitated before slowly moving closer.

"The empress will bring the princesses to see the Doll Palace," a man's voice argued. "The dolls should not just stand there. What good is a palace if the dolls themselves don't look as if they're enjoying it?"

"Just put the dolls inside," Hirata-san advised. "The children who come to see them will make up the stories."

The doll maker must have been talking with the man who would place the American dolls in the giant dollhouse. Chiyo caught her breath. He wanted the dolls in the palace to look as if they were acting out stories. She could help!

She almost called to the men. Then she sank back, pressing closer to the wall. She could think of interesting ways to arrange the dolls in the rooms. But what would the men think of a girl who knocked on the window?

Slowly, she walked to the front of the house and a short distance down the street. The bright yellow parasol shielded Emily Grace and kept rain from the kimono as long as the wind didn't blow. That man must have been the museum curator and Hirata Gouyou's friend, she told herself. If she could find a way to speak to him and suggest stories for the dolls in the palace, surely he would take her past the housekeeper into the house.

She waited for a long time. A few people passed, but no one paid attention to her. Over and over, she imagined words she might say to the man from the museum. She must not shock him by speaking boldly, but she must somehow get him to listen.

The front door opened.

A wiry man in a tunic and dark trousers hurried from the house. Chiyo started toward him, her *geta* clattering on the pavement. The kimono made it hard to move quickly. She wished for her school uniform and shoes.

Wind swept around a corner, hurling rain into her face and wrenching the parasol. When she could look for the man again, he was hailing an approaching streetcar.

A coin flashed as he dropped it into a collection box near the conductor. Chiyo yanked the umbrella down, tucked it under her arm with Emily Grace, and grabbed a handful of her heavy silk kimono. Pulling the material as high as Yaeko's short skirt, she ran for the streetcar. "Wait!" she called. "Please wait for me!"

She clutched a pole by the step as the streetcar began to move and swung aboard, feeling clumsy. The kimono swirled around her ankles, and the bundle shifted in her arms. "Mama," the doll protested through the cloth.

The conductor looked at her. She had one sen

left. Was it enough? She struggled with Emily Grace and the umbrella while groping for the purse she carried inside her obi. She drew out her remaining coin, hesitated, then dropped it in the box.

The conductor glanced at it and turned to his controls.

Weak with relief, Chiyo sank onto the end of a long bench that faced the street. She had managed the first step. Now she must talk to the man from the doll palace. Doubt gripped her again. Could she do that? Would he listen?

For a moment, she kept her eyes down and sat very still, as was expected of a humble young girl. The moment passed. She raised her head and glanced around to see where the man was sitting.

CHAPTER 38

Since the sides of the streetcar were open, rain blew in along with the noise of the street. It felt to Chiyo as if all the people aboard were a group, like a family or a school. They were sharing an adventure. Shouldn't it be permissible to speak to one of them?

The man from the doll palace sat at the other end of the same long bench. Chiyo moved closer. Her heart beat in her throat.

The conductor rang his bell. People climbed on and off. A man and woman came aboard and sat nearby. The woman glanced at her as if she disapproved of a girl traveling alone. Chiyo lowered her eyes, her mind disappointingly empty of ideas.

All she could think of was Mrs. Ogata's list of rules. *No talking with men outside of school and family.*

She had made a mistake. She should not be here. As the streetcar slowed to a stop, she stood. She must leave before she got farther from the doll maker's house. The housekeeper must let her speak with Hirata-san now that his visitor was gone.

The woman next to her stood in the same moment and accidentally bumped the yellow parasol. The bundle slipped. Emily Grace cried, "Mama!" Her arms and legs clattered to the seat and floor of the car.

"Oh!" Chiyo bent to grab for an arm. The man and woman left, the woman's long skirt brushing a doll leg and spinning it toward the street.

Chiyo's hands were full. She looked helplessly after the leg.

The man from the doll palace caught it before it could topple off. He rescued the other leg and arm as Chiyo sank onto the bench with Emily Grace. "*Arigatogozaimasu*," she whispered.

With kindness in his eyes, he said, "I believe we saved them all."

Chiyo opened the bundle, and he placed the arms and legs beside Emily Grace. Despite everything, Emily Grace continued to smile. She was not afraid. The doll's smile reminded Chiyo of Yaeko, who would not hesitate to speak to a kind man.

Softly, Chiyo said, "My doll has an interesting story." Would he remember that he wanted the dolls in the doll palace to act out stories? "But the ending is sad."

Interest filled his eyes. "May I hear her story?"

Chiyo kept her gaze on Emily Grace. Her heart pounded so hard she could almost hear it. "She is one of more than twelve thousand dolls from America. Children there sent them to us."

"Ah, I know of these Dolls of Friendship. So this is one of them." He looked at Chiyo more closely. "You are the girl from the newspaper photograph." He snapped his fingers. "Tamura Chiyo! And this is . . . Emily Grace?"

"*Hai.*" Did he disapprove? She couldn't find the courage—or foolishness—to look into his face for his thoughts, but words pushed past her lips. "The mayor of Tokyo asked me to watch over her."

"The mayor! But how did she lose her arms and legs?"

Chiyo opened the wrappings again to look at the doll. "A jealous girl cut her apart."

The man from the doll palace looked thoughtful. "Can she be fixed?"

"I think so." Chiyo drew in a quick breath. This was the important part of her story. "When I was in Tokyo before, I met a doll maker, Hirata Gouyou-san. I went to his house today to ask if he would help Emily Grace."

"Did he agree?"

Chiyo shook her head. "His housekeeper wouldn't let me talk to him."

"Ah." The curator nodded. "Many people want to meet the doll artist. Sometimes, I'm afraid, Mrs. Sasaki makes decisions for him."

Leaning back, he gazed at the wet street. Chiyo felt her courage fading. She was not a bold flapper. She could not stare into a man's face or argue until he agreed to help.

As Mrs. Ogata's rules began to push back into her mind, the man turned to her again. "I will help you speak to the doll maker, Miss Tamura, but you must also help me. I am Mori Masaru. You may have heard of the great doll palace built for many of the American dolls."

"I have," she exclaimed. She wanted to wriggle with hope and forced herself to sit still.

When he smiled, his eyes crinkled at the corners. "The doll palace will soon be placed in the Educational Museum for all children to see. I am to arrange forty-nine dolls with several Japanese hostess dolls in the house and its gardens, grouped together as if they are enjoying themselves. I wonder if you could help me plan how to arrange them?"

"*Hai!*" She couldn't keep excitement from her voice.

"Excellent! You and I will ride a streetcar back to my friend Hirata Gouyou, and while we travel we will plan how to arrange the little doll ambassadors in the great doll palace."

CHAPTER 39

They left the streetcar and crossed the street, discovering a noodle shop on the far side. With a keen look at Chiyo, Mori-san declared that he was hungry and would be honored to buy her some noodles so that he might enjoy some as well.

Chiyo had not eaten all day. The noodles in the shop were the best she had ever tasted.

When they returned to the doll maker's house, the door opened immediately to Mori-san's knock. Mrs. Sasaki looked out with relief on her face. "Where did you find her?" The housekeeper turned on Chiyo. "You have caused a great deal of worry, miss. Leave that gaudy parasol with your *geta* and come in at once!"

She added to Mori-san, "He has not been able to work since we learned she was missing!"

As hope drove out the cold, Chiyo followed Mrs. Sasaki past a sliding *fusuma* screen into a warm room with hot coals inside a sunken hearth in the center of the floor. A raised table stood over them, with cushions lined along the sides.

"Prepare yourself." Mori-san settled on a cushion beside the warm coals. "I'm afraid we may be about to hear more scolding."

"I didn't know anyone would worry." Chiyo walked back and forth, too nervous to sit down. She stopped at a window where the shoji screen had been pushed aside and looked out at the terrace with raked white rocks beyond. How had the doll maker learned she was missing? "I thought no one in the whole world cared."

"Someone always cares."

My parents care! The thought hit her so suddenly she nearly dropped Emily Grace. Feeling boneless, she sank onto a cushion with the doll in her lap. What if word had reached *Okaasan* and *Otousan*? They would be afraid for her. Disappearing was worse than going to Masako's *omiai*. "I didn't mean to worry anyone. I just wanted help for Emily Grace."

The *fusuma* screen flew open. Hirata-san rushed in. He stopped when he saw Chiyo. "Where have you been, Chiyo-chan? I received a telephone call from the headmaster at your school. I was about to go out and search the streets for you."

Chiyo looked up in surprise. "The school called? Why? They don't want me there."

"They cannot have a girl in their care disappear." The doll maker's eyes became stern. "Your headmaster heard from a nurse at the hospital. She told him she gave you a ride from Toride to my house."

"Yaeko," Chiyo whispered. "She said she would help."

"I had no idea where you were!" His frown deepened. "People might have said the doll maker is too old to paint fine lines. He has made a slave of the girl so she can do his work for him."

Chiyo wished she could slide under the table away from that stern look, even if it would mean sliding onto coals. "You're not old," she said.

Amusement replaced the frown, but he kept his voice stern. "So the rumor would not be true. What is true is that you risked your safety on a dangerous trip. You must never do such a thing again."

"No, Hirata-san." Chiyo heard more than stern

words from the doll maker. She heard that he cared about her. Just as Mori-san had said. She sat in silence with her head bowed, the image of a girl deeply shamed. But inside, she smiled.

Mori-san said patiently, "If you have finished working out your fear for her by scolding the child, will you hear why she came to see you?"

"I would like that."

Carefully, Chiyo placed her bundle on the table. "It's Emily Grace," she said as she unwrapped the doll. "She's hurt. Please, Hirata-san, will you help her?"

He called to the housekeeper for tea, then lowered himself to a cushion beside Chiyo and looked curiously at the doll. Mrs. Sasaki hurried in with a tray.

"Someone cut her all apart," Chiyo explained. "Headmaster was going to throw her away. I didn't know what to do. So I brought her here. Can you . . . can she be fixed?"

The doll maker studied her for a long moment before looking again at the doll. "Perhaps. But tell me, how did this come about?"

Why did people always want to know the bad parts? Why couldn't they see what had to be done and just set about doing it? Chiyo took a deep breath, then went through the whole thing again, as she had told it to Yaeko and, in part, to Mori Masaru.

Hirata-san sipped his tea, glancing occasionally at Emily Grace. At last, he lifted the doll's body and studied the bits of rubber bands still visible in the holes where her arms and legs had been attached. "I have not seen this before. Our dolls with moveable joints have fabric fastening them to the body."

He was going to refuse to help Emily Grace. She could feel it coming. At least he was nicer than his housekeeper. He had let her get warm before sending her away.

"I have no bands such as these in my workshop," he explained.

"No," Chiyo whispered. No, he wouldn't have. He didn't make dolls like Emily Grace. She reached for the doll and began to bundle the coverings around her.

"I will send a boy to locate bands of the right length and weight," the doll maker said. "If none can be found, then lengths of fabric passed through her body may serve to hold the parts together. Either way, repairing her will be interesting."

Chiyo sank back on the cushion. He would help!

He might use fabric lengths. That didn't matter. All that mattered was that Emily Grace would be whole again.

Hirata-san rose to his feet. "First, I must inform your school that you are safe."

"And Miss Tamura is helping me place the dolls." The museum curator removed a scroll from his tunic and spread it on the table.

Chiyo leaned closer to look at the diagram of the two-story doll palace with many rooms. He had shown her parts of it in the noodle house, but she had not seen it spread open. She turned to him in surprise. "This shows a garden with a pond and flowers."

He nodded. "The palace will be mounted on a cabinet so that children may stand at eye level with the dolls." For several minutes, Chiyo leaned over the plan, deciding where dolls might pretend to share tea or stand before a mirror choosing pretty ribbons or enjoy the garden while watching koi in the pond.

At last, Mori Masaru-san rolled up his plans. His smile thanked Chiyo even more than his bow. They had become friends while they planned for the dolls. She was sorry to see him leave.

Mrs. Sasaki came in with a *bento* box and suggested lunch in the garden. Chiyo gathered her sewing kit and the doll's torn dress and followed the housekeeper outside, pleased to see that the rain had stopped. Bright sunlight brought warmth to the terrace.

The housekeeper paused in the doorway. "Hirata-san has questions for you to consider. He asks, what is to become of the doll once she is repaired? Will she be safe when you return her to your school?"

The questions hung in the air with Chiyo while the housekeeper closed the screen, leaving her alone with the raked rocks of the garden.

CHAPTER 40

Chiyo answered in silence. *I spent the mayor's money to bring Emily Grace to Tokyo because the school wanted to throw her in the trash. I may be forbidden to attend Masako's wedding. Emily Grace is mine now, and I'm keeping her with me. Forever!*

Still the doll maker's questions circled like smoke from green wood. She couldn't get away from them. She thought of the mayor placing the protector's medal on its ribbon over her head. The medal was a promise to keep the doll safe for the girls. *All* the girls.

And I tried, she argued silently. *But they called me vain and wouldn't let me stay with her. And Hoshi cut Emily Grace apart.*

Maybe Hirata-san didn't understand. She would explain the danger to Emily Grace when she talked to him again. He must see that the doll should not go back to the school.

She chose a stone bench on the sheltered terrace where she could look out at the raked white rocks. Before taking out her threads and needle, she explored the *bento* box and found rice balls, dried herring, and small pickled salt plums in the divided sections.

When the box was empty, she turned to her sewing. Gradually, the tranquillity of the garden soaked into her. She had no idea how much time passed while she worked on the doll dress. Shadows had grown longer before Hirata-san stepped onto the terrace. "Here is someone to see you."

Chiyo sprang to her feet, dropping the dress to the bench. The doll maker held out Emily Grace, whole again and dressed in a small kimono. The doll's arms reached toward her.

Tears slipped down Chiyo's cheeks as she hugged Emily Grace. "*Arigatogozaimasu,* Hirata-san. *Arigato . . . !*" Her voice broke and she swallowed hard. After choking back tears so often, it was foolish to cry because she was happy!

"Have you forgiven that wicked girl?" Chiyo asked the doll. She imagined Emily Grace's answer. Emily Grace wanted to continue the adventure that had brought her all the way across the Pacific Ocean.

With reluctance, Chiyo answered the question he had asked through the housekeeper. "She will go back to Tsuchiura Girls' School. She came a long way for all the girls there. I must trust Headmaster to keep her safe this time."

"He is sure to do that," the doll maker said gently. "I will drive you to your school before the day grows later."

Chiyo gathered her sewing materials and followed him back into the house. She was to ride in yet another automobile. Secret pleasure warmed her as she imagined the girls' surprise when they saw her arrive.

"The school expects Yamada Nori to come for you late today."

She had forgotten that this was the day Yamada-san was to remove her from the school. But if she left, who would watch over Emily Grace to be sure the school kept the doll safe?

Hirata Gouyou's car was more like Yaeko's than the mayor's big automobile. Chiyo sat in front with the doll maker, holding Emily Grace in her new kimono. As the miles rushed by, Hirata-san asked her about the doll palace. Chiyo was happy to describe each story grouping of dolls she and Mori-san had planned.

Almost before she knew it, they reached Tsuchiura Girls' School. No one was outside to see her arrive, but Yamada Nori's horse stood tethered beside the gate, with the carriage behind it. Chiyo's stomach felt as if her *obi-jime* were tied too tightly around her middle. She had to face questions again. Questions and disapproval.

The sooner she was inside, the sooner she could explain. She must show them how beautiful Emily Grace looked now. Surely Yamada-san would be proud of her for saving the doll.

She hoped he would be proud.

The moment the car stopped, she jumped from it, calling back to Hirata-san, "*Arigatogozaimasu!* I must go." She ran toward the inside courtyard, wondering if Yamada Nori was in Headmaster's office.

The school seemed strange to her, as if she were returning after a long time away. When she stepped inside, it all rushed back and she was on familiar ground.

She stopped, listening. Someone was crying nearby. Hoshi's voice rose above the sobs. "You will say nothing. Nothing!"

CHAPTER 41

Chiyo wanted to rush away from more trouble. But she couldn't go on when someone needed help. The voices came from a small room where the girls ironed fabric for their sewing class. Cautiously, she cracked open the door.

Hoshi stood with her back to the door, gripping the wood handle of an iron heating on a hot stove. Shizuko faced her with tears running down her flushed face.

"They'll ask me," Shizuko said. "They're asking everyone."

"You know nothing."

"You cut the doll. I saw you do it. You put the pieces in Chiyo's desk. I haven't told, but they'll know if they ask."

Was it possible that the headmaster and teachers were trying to learn what had really happened? Shizuko knew all along. The knowledge slammed into Chiyo. That was why Shizuko had acted so strangely when she crawled onto her futon and wouldn't talk.

Inside the sewing room, Hoshi raised the hot iron. "I warned you."

"No!" Shizuko screamed. "Hoshi! Don't!"

Chiyo shoved the door wide. "Hoshi! Stop!"

Hoshi swung around. Her eyes looked like those of a stray dog Chiyo had once seen cornered. She rushed at Chiyo with the raised iron.

Chiyo bent to place Emily Grace safely on the floor. When she sprang up, her head hit Hoshi's elbow. Hoshi's hand swung around. The hot steel seared into her heavy silk kimono. Shrieking, she dropped the iron. The metal plate left its burned shadow in the silk.

Hoshi kept shrieking while Headmaster Hanarai rushed in with Yamada Nori behind him. "What is happening here?"

Yamada-san reached for Chiyo. She turned

to him, unsure whether he would protect her or blame her.

"Look what she did!" Hoshi held out the burned part of her kimono. "My best kimono! Ruined! It's her fault. She ruined it! This school will hear from my father!"

Hirata-san stepped into the room. "It is better to burn a kimono than a girl's face. I saw the entire incident."

Shizuko had cringed back against shelves of fabric. Now she came forward. Her voice shook when she spoke to the headmaster. "Hoshi cut the doll. I saw her do it. She said she would burn me if I told."

Girls crowded the doorway, trying to see in. From beyond them, Kaito-sensei called, "Young ladies, please! Return to your classrooms."

Headmaster Hanarai looked as if a tsunami had washed him from his familiar world to one he didn't know. "It was you, Miss Miyamoto? You damaged the doll? And now you've threatened harm to these girls?"

"Who says that? The doll maker?" Hoshi drew herself straight. "He's her friend. He will say whatever she wants to hear."

Headmaster turned. He looked flushed as he

recognized the master doll maker, who had just been insulted. Bowing, he said, "Hirata Gouyou-san, you honor us with your visit." Flushing even deeper, he added, "*Sumimasen*, the girl is upset. You saw this . . . what happened here?"

"I did." Hirata-san stood solidly in the doorway, making it clear that he meant to be heard.

Headmaster Hanarai glanced at the girls still crowding nearby despite Kaito-sensei's orders. "Go to your classes, all of you."

They scurried away, sounding like pigeons on a roof, asking one another what had happened.

Chiyo picked up Emily Grace and straightened her kimono. She had pictured a grand return with the doll repaired and everyone impressed. Now the others scarcely noticed.

"We will go to my office," Headmaster said. "Gentlemen, this way please. You three, too," he added to Chiyo and the other two girls.

Hoshi shot a warning look at Shizuko, who looked scared but defiant.

"Too late," Chiyo told Hoshi. "Everyone knows."

As Headmaster continued to clear away curious girls, Yamada-san told Chiyo, "You don't have to stay, little sister. We can leave right now."

The offer tempted her. She wanted to leave the school, to let all that had happened fade into the past. She looked at the doll maker. His expression was hard to read, but she felt she knew his thoughts. He believed that she should stay.

"Headmaster may have questions for me," she said, deciding. "And I want to be sure the truth is told."

Hirata-san's eyes warmed with approval. "She is a brave girl," he told Yamada-san. "Brave enough to see this matter through."

Realizing that the men had not met, Chiyo said quickly, "This is the doll artist Hirata Gouyou-san. And this is Yamada Nori-san, who plans to marry my sister."

After all that had happened, she almost expected him to say, "In a thousand years, you could not convince me to marry your sister." But she saw that he had come to support her, not to criticize.

After inviting the men into his office, Headmaster turned. "You three girls wait here. I do not want to hear a sound from any of you."

They each chose a section of wall to wait against. Chiyo stood near Hirata Gouyou's drawing of her, fearing that Hoshi still might try to destroy it.

Hoshi stood as far from Chiyo and Shizuko

as possible, looking as if she had paused there by accident.

At last, Headmaster Hanarai opened the door for Hirata-san. After bowing to the doll maker, Headmaster said, "The school is grateful for your assistance in this matter and for returning our missing student."

Hirata-san returned the bow, then nodded to Chiyo before walking away. Yamada-san left the office after a brief word to Headmaster Hanarai. His nod toward Chiyo was encouraging, but he, too, left the school.

"Come in, please," Headmaster said, motioning to the three of them. They hurried after him into the office and stood in a row before his desk, hands clasped at their waists, eyes lowered.

Headmaster Hanarai sat behind his desk. "Miss Miyamoto, I have talked with your father by telephone. He happens to be in Tsuchiura and is on his way here to discuss whether you will be permitted to remain at this school."

Hoshi's head came up. "Not remain . . . ?"

"You may leave now to go directly home, Miss Miyamoto. I will discuss this further with your father."

Would Hoshi be expelled, too? The possibility

shocked Chiyo almost as much as it had Hoshi. *I'm a nobody from the country,* she told herself. *No one will be surprised to see me leave, but everyone knows that Hoshi practically rules the school.*

How would General Miyamoto react? Chiyo thought of his demands on Hoshi and couldn't help pitying her—a little.

"Hirata Gouyou-san has explained what he heard and saw during the confrontation in the fabric room," Headmaster said to Shizuko. "Your story is not necessary at this time. Be prepared, however, to be called from class if General Miyamoto should wish to hear exactly what you saw done to the doll."

Shizuko bowed and hurried from the office, looking frightened at the thought of General Miyamoto.

Now me. Chiyo braced inwardly, expecting to hear again that she was unwelcome at the school. She wondered if Yamada-san had already offered to remove her.

Headmaster gazed at her for a long moment, as if considering his next words. "Miss Tamura," he said finally, "I hope you understand how much distress you caused by leaving the school without a word to anyone, much less permission."

"*Sumimasen,*" she apologized. "I promised to

protect Emily Grace. I had to save her from the trash. And I was told I was not wanted at this school."

Again, the headmaster let moments pass in silence. "It seems the school owes you an apology," he said at last. "Perhaps our error equals yours."

Their error? An apology? Was she hearing right?

"By arranging repairs to the American doll, you prevented a loss of honor to the school."

Chiyo looked at him, too surprised to keep her eyes modestly lowered. Headmaster's smile might have been thin, but it was there.

"Now that I have the facts, I am rescinding what I said earlier." His gaze met hers. "Yamada Nori believes that you should leave Tsuchiura Girls' School. He does not think us worthy of you. We at the school hope you will stay."

Chiyo's head reeled with the unfairness she had received here, especially the blame for hurting Emily Grace. They should have known she would never do that.

"I understand you may need time to think," Headmaster Hanarai said into her silence. "Yamada-san is waiting to take you into town for tea. I will meet with you when you are ready to make your decision. Are we agreed?"

"*Hai,*" she whispered, while questions and doubts ran through her head. She had expected to leave the school forever. Should she stay? She didn't want to. Yet she did want to. She squeezed her hands together, unable to decide what she wanted.

The decision felt too big for her to make. As she bowed and left the office, angry footsteps pounded down the walkway along the courtyard, all but covering the flutter of girls escaping into nearby rooms.

CHAPTER 42

Chiyo recognized the general's footsteps before he came into sight, walking fast. She flattened against the wall to one side, trying to be invisible.

He strode past without glancing toward her and slammed open the door into Headmaster's office. "When you failed my daughter, you failed me," he roared. The door banged shut.

Chiyo ran as fast as her kimono allowed, to get away from the angry general. Yamada-san would be with his carriage beyond the front gate. She couldn't wait to be in his friendlier company.

The end of her obi swung loose. Her kimono was coming apart, and her hair needed combing. Changing direction, she hurried to the second building and up the stairs to the sleeping area.

To her surprise, Mrs. Ogata held out her arms. "You have been through too much. I see it in your face. Come, let me straighten your obi."

"I have to hurry," Chiyo said, out of breath. "Someone is waiting."

Mrs. Ogata nodded. Her assured manner and capable hands on the obi helped Chiyo breathe more naturally. Yamada-san would still be waiting if she took a little longer. He expected her to be with Headmaster for several minutes.

She combed her hair with hard pulls. Each pull felt as if she combed out memories of the too-short train ride, the drive with Yaeko, the doll maker's stubborn housekeeper, and all the rest of it.

The need to escape eased only when she saw Yamada-san waiting with his carriage.

"You will have no more problems with Miyamoto Hoshi," he told her as he helped her into it. "While I waited here, the general stalked back to his car. He shouted to anyone who would listen that he was removing his daughter. He blames the school for her problems."

Hoshi was gone. The mean tricks would end. It was hard to believe. "The school will be different without her," Chiyo murmured. *In a new school, Hoshi will be the outsider and others may be mean to her.* The thought was unkind, but Chiyo couldn't feel kind toward Hoshi.

I should wish her well, she scolded herself, but added fiercely, *I'm glad I don't have to.*

"I understand his fury," Yamada-san continued, as if unaware of the thoughts raging through Chiyo. "The school has also failed you."

That was true, but she had never expected to hear someone say so. "They wouldn't let me keep my promise to the mayor." That hurt almost as much as seeing Emily Grace cut into pieces. That, and being blamed for cutting her.

There was so much more she could say to Yamada Nori, but she told herself it was over now. Keeping bitterness in her heart would be the same as letting Hoshi win, but it was hard to let the anger go, even with Headmaster's apology and the knowledge that Hoshi would never return to the school.

Yamada-san drove his carriage to a teahouse where windows allowed a view of a stream rippling over stones. Chiyo sat on a firm cushion beside a low table while a *shamisen* and a koto played somewhere unseen. She wanted to stare around with wide eyes. Must she still be as well mannered as Hoshi? Aware that Yamada-san watched her with amusement, she concentrated on the lotus blossoms in the center of the table and began to feel soothed by the flowers' creamy whiteness.

"You have had an adventurous day," Yamada-san told her after discussing choices with a kimono-clad attendant. "I would like to hear how you managed to reach Tokyo by yourself."

She had expected it, yet the question was like a boulder thrown into the tranquil scene. The trip to Tokyo flew through her head. None of it had been the behavior of a modest traditional girl. Nothing about that trip could please Yamada Nori.

He waited for her answer.

"I . . . I rode the train." She would not be like Hoshi and hide the truth. "I lost the money you gave me for the first trip. It was an accident."

Yamada-san waited, but she felt he was putting

questions aside for later. She no longer felt tranquillity from the lotus blossoms.

"I had just enough yen to go to Toride," she finished in a hurry. "I thought I could ask for a ride with a farmer on his way to the market in Tokyo."

Yamada-san sounded as if he were trying to stay calm. "Did you find such a farmer?"

"No." She twisted a tassel on one corner of the cushion. "I was too late. They had all gone."

The attendant returned to pour fragrant green tea while Chiyo tried to sit quietly. Had she ruined Masako's chance for marriage? How would she face her sister?

Yamada-san sipped his tea. "The farmers had gone. Yet you reached Tokyo."

Chiyo blocked the word *flapper* from her lips before it could slip out. She knew he would not approve of riding with a flapper. "A nurse stopped her automobile to ask if I needed help. I told her I had to get Emily Grace repaired. So she drove me."

She raised her eyes to Yamada-san, unable to keep them humbly lowered. "I promised the mayor of Tokyo that I would take care of her."

Yamada-san ignored the last to ask, "The nurse would be the woman who later called the school?"

Chiyo heard the expected disapproval and said quietly, "She was very nice."

"At your request, Hirata Gouyou repaired the doll?"

"*Hai,*" she agreed hesitantly. Yamada-san heard the hesitation and looked questioningly over his teacup. Telling it all could make things worse, but secrets always came out.

She spoke quickly, lining up the details like ducks on a pond. "First I met the man who is to arrange American dolls in the big doll palace the empress ordered. He said he would help me see the doll maker if I would help him decide how to arrange the dolls in the palace. So I did that while Hirata-san repaired Emily Grace."

She took a deep breath, feeling dizzy, while Yamada-san gazed thoughtfully into his teacup. After a long moment, he shook his head. "You took a dangerous risk in waiting on the road for a ride and by accepting one."

"*Hai,*" she admitted. "I had hoped for a farm cart—"

He cut her off. "You also took a risk in talking

to a man who must have been unknown to you. It is time to return home to the care of those who love you."

That was what she had wanted from the start. She had wanted to go home before she was a wheel's turn away.

Yet she saw again the fierceness in *Okaasan*'s eyes when it had been so desperately hard to leave. "Put fear behind," her mother had insisted. "Seize this opportunity." How could she leave the school after so short a time there?

Yamada-san's voice became firm after waiting for her answer and receiving none. "You will be happier in your old school in the village. Your friends will welcome you."

"I would like to see Yumi and her sister." But there was more to learn in Tsuchiura. She would never have made the trip to Tokyo if she had remained at home, never have ridden in an automobile or on a streetcar. She would never have met the doll maker, the mayor, the man from the doll palace . . . or Yaeko.

"You are frowning," Yamada-san said quietly.

"The nurse . . . her name was Yaeko . . . she said that school in Tsuchiura would change me, that it had already. I think she was right."

"You do not wish to return to the village school?" His brows rose, then he nodded. "I understand. Headmaster Hanarai said that you are having trouble with your schoolwork. You have been too often away from classes. You would feel shame in returning to your old school when you are behind your friends in their lessons."

Chiyo didn't think she would be behind. The school in Tsuchiura was ahead of the village school. That had been her problem. Yet she had missed many classes.

Yamada-san was looking at her with decision in his face. "I will arrange for a private tutor in your home."

Private lessons! Without Hoshi to make trouble. "Could Yumi come, too?"

"Of course. You will enjoy learning together. Is it settled, then?"

She wanted so badly to say "*Hai*, it is settled. I will go back to the village and study with a private tutor." How grand that sounded. And yet, it sounded lonely, too. For all her problems in Tsuchiura, she would miss everyone there, especially Hana, with her teasing eyes and quick humor.

It would be good to see Yumi again. But Yumi

might not want to leave her friends at the village school for a private tutor. Worse, if she left Tsuchiura, Chiyo knew she would be turning away from *Okaasan*'s hopes.

And what about Emily Grace? She would have to leave the doll behind. Emily Grace belonged to the school. Hoshi would be gone, but someone else might feel as she did or want revenge for Hoshi.

If she stayed, Yamada-san might be angry.

"Tears?" he exclaimed. "Why is this?"

Words burst from Chiyo. "Masako wants to marry you. I'm afraid I will ruin her life."

"How could you . . ." His voice trailed off. "Chiyo-chan, where you go to school has nothing to do with your sister. We will marry, if she is willing."

"My family said I had to learn to be modest and not shame you."

Yamada-san set down his cup. "Chiyo, listen to me. I was impressed by your adventurous spirit. I wanted to give you opportunities to grow that you would not find in the small village school. That is why I brought you to Tsuchiura. You should stay only if you wish it."

Chiyo rubbed tears from her cheeks. Could it

be true? Had he sent her to the expensive school because he thought it would be better for her, not because her behavior shamed Masako?

She felt his gaze on her face, though now she remembered to keep her eyes lowered as she murmured, "*Arigatogozaimasu.*"

"Perhaps," he mused, "school here was not the best choice. You are young yet, and missing your family." After a long moment of silence, she risked a glance at him and saw decision come into his face.

"I will be in Tokyo on business for several days," he said. "Prepare to return home when I return. I will provide a tutor to help with those classes where you are behind. You will help your sister prepare for her wedding."

"I would like that." Was he making the decision for her? He seemed certain she wanted to return home to stay, when she was not certain.

"The new term will begin in Tsuchiura after the wedding. By then, you will have had time enough to think everything through. You may decide whether to return here or stay with your family."

She could choose to come back! She was to help

with the wedding. Only afterward must she decide whether to try again to fit in with the others in Tsuchiura Girls' School.

This time when she said "*Arigatogozaimasu,*" she meant her thanks with all her heart.

CHAPTER 43

When Chiyo came into the classroom the next morning, Hoshi was not present, but Shizuko was, looking pale and staring at her desk.

Kaito-sensei rang her bell for silence. "You are all aware of the recent unpleasantness. There is no need to go into details. Miyamoto Hoshi is no longer a student in this school. Perhaps you are wondering why Sakamoto Shizuko is in class. You are asking if failure to report a crime should also demand punishment."

"It isn't fair," said a girl from across the room. "Chiyo was told to leave when Headmaster just *thought* she hurt the doll."

Chiyo looked at the girl in surprise. What was it that Mori-san had said in Tokyo? *Someone always cares.*

"Headmaster Hanarai believes—we all believe—it is best for Miss Sakamoto and for the school to allow her to remain with us." Kaito-sensei had to ring her bell again to silence indignant whispers. "However . . . *However* . . ."

Everyone became silent, eager to hear what awful fate awaited Shizuko.

Kaito-sensei looked sternly at Shizuko. "Miss Sakamoto will apologize publicly to Miss Tamura."

That was all? Chiyo's head roared with protest. She thought of the station agent who insisted on more yen than she had and of reaching Toride too late to ask for a ride with a farmer. She thought of standing in the rain outside the doll maker's home when his housekeeper refused to admit her. She thought of running for the streetcar when she didn't know if one sen was enough to ride and of daring to speak to a strange man.

She would not have had to make that scary trip alone to Tokyo if Shizuko had simply told the teachers that it was Hoshi who had cut the doll apart. Most of all, she would not have been the one accused, shamed, and told to leave the school.

Everyone was looking at her, waiting for her to protest, to say that an apology wasn't enough.

"It's not fair," the girl near the far wall said again. All around the room, other girls murmured agreement.

Who was the girl who spoke first? Chiyo wondered, then remembered her name, Michi. She was the one who had missed the trip to Tokyo. *If I stay in Tsuchiura Girls' School, I want to know Michi better.*

The nurse had said that the world was Chiyo's oyster and that she had the nerve to swallow it whole. Even the pearl. *She should have said even the hard, rough shell,* Chiyo told herself while Kaito-sensei called the whispering students to order.

On her way into class, she had glimpsed Emily Grace inside Headmaster's office on a stand near his desk. The doll still wore her kimono. She looked beautiful, with her bright blue eyes and eager smile. *Emily Grace would want me to say I forgive Shizuko.*

Chiyo could not say something she didn't feel.

"Miss Sakamoto?" Kaito-sensei prompted.

Shizuko rose slowly from her desk. She walked to the front of the room and placed her hands at her waist, bowing over them. "I have wronged you,

Miss Tamura. I have wronged Emily Grace. I have wronged my school."

Her voice wavered, and she slipped to her knees, bowing forward until her forehead pressed the floor. "I let fear stop me from telling the truth. *Sumimasen,* Miss Tamura," she said, as if Chiyo were her superior. "I am very, very sorry."

Chiyo felt Shizuko's shame in her own heart. She came to her feet and went to her. Dropping to her knees, she put her hands on the girl's arms and urged her to stand. "I was afraid of Hoshi, too. Many of us were."

As she rose with Shizuko, Chiyo felt everyone looking at her, waiting for her to say more. Maybe they wondered if she would say that Shizuko was forgiven.

She imagined Emily Grace looking at her, too, waiting for an answer. What she said next could make a difference if she came back after Masako's wedding.

If not for Shizuko's silence, I would have missed so much. The trip to Tokyo alone had started out scary, but it had become exciting. She thought of the nurse who had driven her from Toride. How was Yaeko different from Masako? It wasn't her short skirt or breezy talk. It was her education. A doctor wanted to marry Yaeko, but she was resisting. She would make up her mind when she was ready, not when anyone else told her she was ready.

Maybe I will marry when I reach my sister's age, but only if I wish to, Chiyo told herself. Everything else vanished in a rush of excitement.

Masako may choose me to hold up the long white kimono she will wear for the ceremony. I will be there when she changes into a colorful one for the reception to show she is ready for everyday life, and then into the party dress she will wear to celebrate with family and friends.

I will tease her about the nine sips of sake from three different cups she and her new husband must exchange to enjoy triple happiness in their marriage. When the celebrating was over, Chiyo knew she would return to Tsuchiura Girls' School. *With an education, I will have choices. I will choose my own future.*

For the few days remaining in the school term, she would work hard to learn all she could. There was no time to cling to hard feelings. "Kaito-sensei, may I speak to the class?"

"Of course, Miss Tamura. What is it?"

As everyone's eyes turned toward her, Chiyo stood a little straighter. "I wish to share the haiku a girl in America sent with our doll. I mean to remember these words and their hope for peace. I hope all of us will." She drew a steadying breath, then repeated the haiku in a clear voice.

"Emily Grace glows.
Her warm smile carries friendship.
Sunlight after rain."

As everyone murmured approval, Chiyo turned to Shizuko, letting her smile accept the girl's apology and invite her friendship.

AUTHOR'S NOTE

A few years ago, pictures of my little granddaughter dressed in a beautiful kimono led me to research the Japanese Girls' Day festival called Hinamatsuri, where treasured dolls are put on display. That research led to the all-but-forgotten Friendship Dolls project of 1926 and eventually to my novel *Ship of Dolls* and to telling more of the story through the eyes of a Japanese girl in *Dolls of Hope.*

In 1926, Dr. Sidney Gulick, a teacher missionary who retired after working in Japan for thirty years, worried about approaching war between the two countries he loved. He began the Friendship

Doll project, urging children across America to send thousands of dolls to children in Japan in hope of creating friendship between the two countries. Children in nearly every state responded. The "Blue-Eyed Dolls" received an enthusiastic welcome in Japan, with parties and ceremonies held throughout the country. Children there donated money to have fifty-eight large dolls created by their country's finest doll makers and dressed in rich kimonos. These, with many accessories, were sent in gratitude to children in America in time for Christmas of 1927.

Sadly, the beautiful hope for friendship expressed by the children of both countries could not prevent war. With the Japanese bombing of American ships in Pearl Harbor in 1941, America was drawn into World War II. In both countries, the dolls became symbols of the enemy. The Japanese government ordered the American dolls to be destroyed. In America, the Japanese dolls were put into storage and forgotten.

Now, long after WWII, the two countries have healed and become friends. The friendship project lives on as well, with dolls again sharing the culture of each country.

Bill Gordon's website on the Friendship Dolls,

www.bill-gordon.net/dolls, provided a major source of information for the novels, with photos and facts from 1926 to today.

Doll maker Hirata Gouyou really lived and created some of the Dolls of Return Gratitude, including one I have visited in a museum at the University of Nevada in Reno. Hirata Gouyou, who eventually became one of Japan's revered Living Treasures, was a young man of twenty-four and already a master doll maker in 1927. If Chiyo had been real instead of a fictional character, I believe she would have enjoyed knowing Hirata-san, just as I have enjoyed giving him an important part in the story.

The value of the Japanese yen has fallen dramatically since WWII. In Chiyo's time, one yen was worth about fifty cents in U.S. money. Chiyo's two 10-yen coins from the mayor of Tokyo were together worth about $10.00 in U.S. money. Of course, prices in 1927 were much lower than today, and to Chiyo that amount was a fortune. She rarely had even a sen, worth about 1/100th the value of one yen, as a penny is worth 1/100th of a U.S. dollar.

For research on life in rural Japan in 1927, I relied on a fascinating collection of interviews in the book *Memories of Silk and Straw: A Self-Portrait of Small-Town Japan* by Dr. Junichi Saga. And I am indebted to my daughter-in-law, Miwa, for researching Japanese-language Internet sites for information needed for the story and for help with cultural descriptions and occasional words in the Japanese language. Writing Chiyo's story has been a challenge, an adventure, and a joy. Any mistakes that may have slipped through are entirely my own.

GLOSSARY

People

-chan: used after a name (usually a child's) to show affection

Okaasama: formal version, mother

Okaasan: mother

Otousama: formal version, father

Otousan: father

Samurai: warrior

-san: used after a name to show respect

Sensei: teacher

Shogun: early military commander appointed by the emperor

Clothing

Geta: wooden clogs raised on platform soles

Kimono: long robe with wide sleeves

Obi: broad band around waist of kimono tied with large bow in back

Obi-jime: narrow tie to hold obi in place and support the bow

Dolls

Gofun: oyster shell mixture to cover doll's face and hands

Hinamatsuri: girls' festival with treasured sets of dolls including emperor, empress, and court

Hina ningyo: human-like doll for girls' festival

Kokeshi: limbless cylindrical wooden doll with painted kimono and round head

Torei Ningyo: Dolls of Return Gratitude

House

Fusuma screen: sliding door used to separate rooms

Koto: stringed musical instrument held flat to play

Shoji screen: a light sliding door or window made of translucent paper over wood frame

Tatami: floor mat woven of rice stems

Expressions

Arigato: thank you

Arigatogozaimasu: more formal, thank you very much

Gomen: casual apology, sorry

Gomenasai: apology, I'm sorry

Hai: yes

Konnichiwa: good afternoon

Sumimasen: formal apology used for older people or superiors

Miscellaneous

Bento box: lunch box

Futon: padded mattress with heavy cover that can be folded away during the day

Haiku: a three-line poem with five syllables in the first line, seven in the second, and five in the third

Hara-kiri: formal suicide with sword

Kanji: characters used in written Japanese

Omiai: an arranged meeting where a couple to be married may meet for the first time

Shamisen: three-stringed musical instrument resembling a lute

Tsunami: enormous ocean surge, usually due to earthquake; can be devastating

Yen, Rin, Sen: early forms of money, with yen the most valuable; rin and sen are no longer used